The Para
Daughter

By Tara Lyons

Print ISBN 978-1-912986-28-6

Also by Tara Lyons

The DI Hamilton Series
In The Shadows (Book 1)
No Safe Home (Book 2)
Deadly Friendship (Book 3)
The Stranger Within (Book 4)

For Laura
My personal paramedic, always on hand to navigate me through the technical side of things, and my cheerleader from the start.

Prologue

The first time a stranger died in my arms, I cried myself to sleep for a week. It doesn't matter what you've learnt, or who they are, or the circumstances that led you both to that point. What matters is that you didn't save them. And it's your job to save them. It's my job.

This was always what I wanted to do with my life. It was my calling – like a nun, I suppose, but without any religious connotation. I'm not a religious person, though I was raised as a Catholic and went to a Catholic school, but when the time comes to choose for yourself, you have to determine what kind of person you are… and want to be. I've seen so much death and destruction in my life, it's hard to believe any god, any almighty being, could make a world where there is so much pain and tragedy and suffering – a lot of which is caused largely by human conflict. But I'm not here to preach.

Anyway, it started for me in 1983 when I broke my ankle. The potential frailty of the human body is what first attracted me, and over the years my fascination flourished steadily. As I grew into a woman, I soon became interested in people as much as with medical science.

Why do we cry when we see blood, even if we don't feel any pain?

Why do people punch and kick others, delighted when they summon a bruise to the flesh or even knock them clean out?

How can some people walk away from a four-car collision with merely a scratch, but others can innocently trip over, bang their head and die instantly?

How do cancer and dementia and multiple sclerosis attack people's bodies in such different ways that it gives each of them a completely unique quality – or lack thereof – of life?

Most importantly, by the age of eighteen, I wanted to know: what can I do to help?

And that was it, that was my calling. I knew I wanted to be in the middle of the storm, rescuing people who couldn't save themselves, bandaging up the wounded and sending them on their merry way again, bringing babies into the world when their mummies couldn't make it to the hospital after their waters broke in the local supermarket, and helping an elderly person after a fall.

It all sounds so easy, with happy endings worthy of any big-stage musical, doesn't it? To believe that I could save the world one 999 call at a time. That was teenager Abi, the one who saw the good in people, the one who believed all bad things happened accidentally. I could cope with looking at and handling the blood and broken bones, the tears and seeping flesh, therefore I could deal with it all. But it's amazing the clarity that comes with just being on the job for one week. Not the years of studying and exams, but that first week of shadowing a team of two in an ambulance.

No amount of medical training prepares you for the crime scenes: the beaten children, the raped women, the boys gunned down. No amount of CPR practice prepares you for the heartache: the stillborns, the suicides, the mental health patients who have no one to turn to and, more often than not, nowhere to go. No amount of experience prepares you for the everyday juggling of emotions that comes with interacting with a multitude of people in London, a city tiptoeing on the edge of crumbling as the National Health Service calls out for help.

And no amount of professionalism trains you for the personal tragedy you're yet to face. When you're used to rescuing people, and then your world comes crashing down around you, who rescues you? When your actions cause devastation to others, and you find yourself all alone, who saves the paramedic?

Chapter one

I jump in the driver's seat and start the engine while Adele takes the details of our next call-out. We've only been on duty for three hours, but we've already had two jobs and couldn't assist with a further eight – such is the way on a daily basis in London. I take a left out of our base, Camden Ambulance Station, and flip on the blues as I turn right on Fleet Road. The swirling emergency lights and piercing buzz of the siren captures everyone's attention and has the desired effect; cars immediately veer to the right and give me a clear passage down the narrow road.

When I first started this job, it amazed me the power my ambulance held as I cruised through the city. Pedestrians would stop to see which direction I was headed in, perhaps worried for their own family – as so many are when they hear the call of the sirens – and cars would go out of their way to mount the kerb, so as not to hold me up en route to my next patient. But, almost seventeen years later, the amazement has faded slightly – not least because I've come across some arseholes who refuse to move out of the way. How would they feel if it were their mother, father or child we were trying to save? I am eternally grateful to those who do their best to let us get through. Like today, dashing past Hampstead Underground tube station and then on towards sheltered accommodation on Hollycroft Avenue. We're just seven minutes out from tending to an elderly man, living alone, who fell in his kitchen.

'So, Abi, any romances started that I should know about?' Adele nonchalantly asks as I manoeuvre through the high street.

Rolling my eyes, I reply, 'Not since you last asked me two days ago.'

'Well, you know, I can't keep up with such a social butterfly as yourself.' I chortle at the sarcasm, but she continues anyway. 'Hot dates here, parties there. How do you find the time for these shifts?'

'Can we not have another day taking the piss out of my social life?'

'Non-existent social life, you mean,' Adele replies, and, from the corner of my eye, I see the huge smile on her face. 'I'm sorry. You know I'm winding you up. I just think you need to get out there and enjoy life.'

Adele's words come from a place of love and friendship, but I can't stifle my frown. 'I do have a life,' I protest, but begin to stutter. 'I-I mean, I do enjoy life. But I have a child, Adele, and Rose is my world. *She's* my life.'

She sucks the air through her teeth and folds her arms. 'Woman, please. Your *child* is a full-grown adult and enjoying her own life at university. You should take a leaf out of her book. She probably goes on more dates than you.'

Probably, I echo in my mind. *More like definitely*. But I don't have time to voice my thoughts as our attention is diverted to the call-out on our radio.

'Change of plan. We have to get over to Regent's Park,' Adele calls out.

'Our ETA is one minute to the old chap on Hollycroft Avenue,' I reply, knowing in my heart there's no point. It's not the first job we've been called away from because a higher priority emergency came through; there's just not enough of us to meet the demand of the calls.

'Patient at Hollycroft is breathing and on the line with one of our operators.' The dispatcher's voice comes through the radio clearly. 'You're needed on Park Road, The London Central Mosque. Tango Alpha.'

'Shit,' I whisper at the operator's use of code.

In the London Ambulance Service, we use a secret set of codes when communicating with one another. Some are used as warnings for what we can expect when we arrive at a scene. Tango Alpha – or TA – is a code we all know well… and one we all hope we never have to hear.

I pull a sharp U-turn in the middle of the road, aware of my personal mobile vibrating against my thigh. I ignore it and slam my foot on the accelerator to race down Finchley Road. The built-up traffic makes the journey slightly difficult here, despite the effort of fellow drivers to move, and our ETA to the scene of the terrorist attack is currently thirteen minutes.

Once Adele has updated our movements, she uses the iPad to familiarise us with the breaking news. Given the location, and the current state of affairs in London, it's sadly no surprise to learn that a suspected terrorist has hit the city.

'And so, the mosque is our rendezvous point for the TA. So that's where it all started?' I ask, making an assumption.

Adele mumbles incoherently for a few moments, reading over the news article and even watching a short clip that has already been posted on YouTube. While waiting, I notice my fingers have gripped the steering wheel so tightly that my pointy white knuckles look as though they're ready to break through my skin.

'Hmm… no, looks like that's where the TA ended,' she finally answers. 'A bomb exploded at Baker Street Underground Station and the suspect was seen fleeing the scene in a white van, speeding away into oncoming traffic, before crashing at Hanover Gate just yards short of the mosque…'

Adele's voice trails off, and we're both left to our thoughts about the potential victims at the scene. The fact we're being sent to the mosque means crews have already been deployed to the Underground station. My heartbeat increases, and I gently tap on the van's horn. The traffic parts and I'm suddenly aware of how dry my mouth is. Attending any crime scene is horrific, but this… this racing into the dangerous unknown, so blind to the terrors you're about to face… I have no words for it.

Park Road, a usually busy and built-up street in London, already resembles a ghost town and it feels eerily quiet as I slow down the van. A uniformed police officer stands in front of a strip of crime-scene tape laced from one side of the street to the other. Cars have been abandoned and pedestrians are peppered along the pavement; some are sat on the kerb crying. Despite the window being open, I can't hear them. Others are huddling into each other, their faces pale and eyes wide and red-rimmed.

We've entered the aftermath.

'Continue on,' Adele instructs, and drags me from my personal reverie.

I turn to her, realising my foot had automatically slid across to the brake and she's already spoken to the uniformed officer stood at the passenger window. The tape is pulled back, and we're directed from officer to officer, their hand signals urging us forward, until we can turn left at Hanover Gate.

An orchestra of sound comes back to me, crashing into my ears like an angry ocean: distant sirens, a woman crying, commands shouted, the metal clink of a rifle, a helicopter's blades roaring overhead. There's one voice that blasts through it all, like a beacon. He details the scene and instructs us that it's safe to move forward and do our jobs. There are two men on the ground. Both have been shot. A surge of adrenaline pumps itself through my veins and my body moves into automatic action without a second thought.

As we're the first crew on the scene, Adele should stay with the van and report back while I triage both patients – prioritising who needs help first. But after quickly assessing the situation, and the obvious need for urgency, I ignore protocol.

'Take the victim closest to us,' I instruct Adele as we both grab our response bags from the ambulance. 'I'll check the status of the one furthest from us, near the mosque entrance.'

She gives me a sharp nod and disappears without a word. The repeated vibration against my leg is distracting and, as I turn and walk back along the side of the van, I pull my mobile from my pocket. Rose's name glares at me, just as I can imagine my only daughter glaring at me while she impatiently waits for an answer. Her worry must be immense, I get that, but I don't have the time to reassure her just yet. I sling the phone onto the passenger seat, slam the door shut and run double time to the blood-soaked body lying thirty or so feet away from me.

Chapter two

The police have cleared the area of any danger. I know that to be a fact, because they wouldn't have let us this far into the crime scene if they hadn't. They have a duty of care to us before we can attempt to save anyone's life. Despite that knowledge, I'm on edge as I work on my patient. Although my hands don't shake as I cut away at his cloak – a long item of clothing that was obviously once a brilliant shade of white but has now been tainted crimson with his blood – there is a sensation in me that builds and builds, like cement filling my organs. I can't help taking deep breaths, slowly inhaling and exhaling as I tend to the male victim's injuries.

The multiple gunshots to his stomach mean my gloved hands are already covered in his blood. With him lying on his back, it's difficult to tell if there are any exit wounds. I can count at least three entry wounds. There are probably more. The victim's guttural groans bring my attention to his face, to his eyes rolling into the back of their sockets and his lips moving. I crouch closer to him, trying to make out what he's whispering, and that's when I notice the marksman, dressed in a black bulletproof uniform, with a rifle aimed at me and my patient.

'Don't help me.' The man on the ground grabs me and murmurs into my ear, his lips grazing against it.

'Sorry, sir?'

'I am… supposed to die. It is my destiny,' he says, and releases the hold he has on my shirt.

As my patient begins to lose consciousness, his eyelids slowly fluttering open and closed, my hands mechanically mop away what I can of the gushing blood and I tend to his injuries. I dress the gunshot wounds as best I can, now counting five spread around his abdomen and chest – it's a wonder he's still alive at all. I grab an oxygen mask from my bag, pull at the elastic strap and move to place it over his head. He grabs my wrist. A collective gasp from the surrounding crowd echoes around me and I hear the metallic clinks of more than one cocking-lever being made ready from the rifles around me. It's also in that moment I notice there's more than one weapon trained on us.

'L-l-leave me,' my patient groans.

I hold my hand up to the nearest SWAT officer. The patient isn't a threat; the lack of grip and force his fingers have on my wrist tells me that much. I know it's their job, but if I can help defuse the tension as much as possible, it will allow me to do mine more effectively. There are so many faces staring at me. I turn around to find the only one I want, and there it is, running towards me.

Another crew have arrived on the scene and Adele's legging it towards me. She says nothing of her patient and listens carefully while I relate the information about mine, before running back to the ambulance for further kit – including a stretcher. We need to get this man off the ground and into an operating theatre if there's going to be any hope of survival for him.

Turning my attention back to my patient, I witness him taking his last breath. It's easy to hear. Easy to me, anyway. This ain't my first rodeo, after all. It's a sound that can haunt you, if you let it. As if the body knows it's the last time it'll ever inhale that invisible life-giving air, and so it vibrates through the chest and gurgles up the throat, until it ends in a death rattle that then becomes so peacefully quiet it could break your soul.

Adele crashes to her knees next to me and with our hands poised we begin CPR.

* * *

Five hours after we first left, Adele and I are back where we started. Camden Ambulance Station. Our base. We were escorted to the hospital by the police, once my patient was breathing again.

The officers never left our side the entire time we were with the patient. On the journey back to base, I learned that Adele's patient – a Metropolitan Police Officer – died at the scene from a single gunshot right through the heart, and my patient was the suspected terrorist. Isn't that unfair? I think I knew those details all along, but it was good to hear Adele's voice saying them out loud. Made everything feel real. It's easy to get so caught up in a job that afterwards, when the pace of everything resets itself, you're vulnerable to forgetting what actually just happened. It's working in the blur – that's what Adele and I call it – a dream-like state, as if you're submerged in water yet still a fully functional human being. So, from time to time, we need each other to pull the other one from the undercurrent and remind ourselves it was real.

My body is aching. Every part of my skull is telling me my slicked-back ponytail is now too tight. My throat hurts when I swallow, as though it's been cut with hundreds of tiny shards of glass. I climb down from the ambulance anyway, knowing the van has to be restocked. A debrief will be scheduled and a statement will be taken also.

'Well, well, if it isn't the Double A Team.'

I smile at Adele when I hear the voice from behind. She rolls her eyes. We both know who it is without even looking, and we both lean against the side of the van for support. It's a nickname that Dave has used for the pair of us since he joined the station four years ago. Even his promotion to manager didn't see him quell the habit. To him, Abi and Adele are the Double A Team. If I'm honest, I kinda like it, but then I like action films. Adele does not. So I pretend to hate it as much as she does.

'I need a drink,' Adele says as Dave approaches the van.

He waits until she's in the building and then asks, 'Is she okay?'

I shrug my shoulders and nod my head at the same time.

'Are you okay, Abi?'

I repeat the actions, this time adding a half-sigh, half-laugh sound.

Dave nods. He understands. Sometimes, words aren't needed between paramedics. We just get that some things we deal with are hard. Really fucking hard.

But, not one to totally ignore a situation – and I guess the fact that he is my manager has something to do with it – Dave lightly places a hand on my shoulder. 'A lot of people wouldn't have been able to do what you did today, Abi. Hell, I dunno if I could have done it in all honesty.'

'Stop fishing for compliments, Dave.' I sigh but smile at the same time. 'You would have, just like any member of our crew would have. It's our job. We don't discriminate.'

'Yeah, but innocent people died today.'

I straighten up and fold my arms. He removes his hand from me and places them both in his pockets. 'Has there been a total fatality count yet?' I ask, unsure if I really want the answer.

'The last count was ten. That includes people at the Underground station and the police officer at the mosque. Those injured… they're still counting.'

I look to the ground and nod. He has the actual numbers, statistics, and information, I know he does. He also knows I don't need the specifics at this exact moment in time. The fact that I'm the one responsible for saving the terrorist who snatched all the lives of those innocent people… well, let's say it's enough to occupy my mind for now.

'You look wrecked.' Dave breaks through my thoughts.

'I said we don't discriminate…' I can't help hesitating; whether it's because I can't find the words immediately or I don't want to admit it, I'm not entirely sure. 'I never said it wasn't difficult.'

Dave's blue eyes bore into mine and, for a moment, I think I can see my own sadness reflected in them, so I look away.

'You and Adele go and change, grab your personal belongings from inside and head home.'

'But we still have to–'

It's not just his hand flying up in front of my face that halts me mid-sentence, I actually don't want to fight his offer.

'I'll take care of the van and, if you both promise to come back first thing in the morning, we'll deal with all the paperwork then.'

'Doesn't protocol demand everything is handled immediately after the incident?'

Dave folds his arms over his chest and almost pouts; it makes me smile. 'Protocol also states that the decision is to be made at the manager's discretion when we're faced with situations like this. All members of my team are different and react differently. You look like a zombie and I can't jeopardise the restocking of one of my ambulances.'

There's a twitch of a smile as he winks at me and I hold my hands up in surrender. Adele comes out of the station with two bottles of water.

'Right, let's do this,' she says; her words are those of fighting talk, but her tone is that of a wounded soldier.

I grab her by the shoulders and spin her around. 'Shh, don't say another word. Dave's tidying up. We're going home. Leave everything where it is in that van.'

Chapter three

Rose Quinn lowers her backside against the hard oak table and folds her arms. She watches him move across the office, lock the door and turn back to face her. His crystal blue eyes cause a shiver to snake down her back, the power of it almost lifting her from her position, and she inhales sharply. The grin on his face tells her that he heard.

He doesn't move. Teasing and testing her as always. Rose can hardly breath with the indecision of what she should do, a tightness in her chest, filling her lungs in an enticing and exciting way, rather than a strangling grip. *How can one man hold so much power over me?* Rose wonders as he slowly takes a step towards her.

The pain in her chest deepens as he approaches, creeping slowly inch by inch, until he's so close she can feel the warmth of his breath on her face. He doesn't touch her. The smirk on his face and the control in his eyes remains. Tempting her. Daring her.

A voice in Rose's head screams, tells her to run for the door, to run from him and end this before it truly begins. In her mind, she knows something has already begun. From the moment they shared their first passionate kiss it was too late. Can she really ignore her feelings? Lustful feelings, maybe… but the pull towards him is so strong. Although she finds it difficult to ignore the screeching warning in her mind, another part of her wants to rip open his shirt. She wants to feel his warm skin under her hands, feel his pink lips against her mouth, her neck, her–

'Stop denying yourself, Rose.' His deep voice breaks through her wicked thoughts.

'I shouldn't have come here,' she whispers, and attempts to clear her throat before continuing; the last thing she wants is to sound vulnerable in front of him. 'And you shouldn't be tempting me.'

Rose curses herself as his lips spread wider in a full smile. She's given too much away. He knows how much she wants him. *But then, he probably always has known*, she thinks, and the internal warning rings louder.

'I'm tempting you, am I?'

She makes an O with her mouth and slowly exhales. 'You shouldn't have asked me to meet you here.'

'But you came.'

'To tell you this has to stop.'

'We haven't started anything... yet.'

Rose slumps; his voice is smooth, what she would imagine warm trickling honey to sound like – should it ever be able to make a noise, of course – and the tightness in the air only serves to confuse her further. Just as she feels the invisible fog is about to wash over her and suck her under, he touches her. His hand on her waist, so soft and delicate, yanks her from his spell and she stands up; he takes her movement as an advance and pulls her closer to his body. She feels his erection prod into her thigh.

'Stop,' she demands, and places her hand on his chest. When he doesn't move, she shoves him just hard enough to place a small amount of distance between them. 'This will not happen.'

The smile fades from his face. 'You want it just as much as I do.'

'No.' The warning voice in Rose's mind finally outweighs the lustful thoughts. She feels ashamed of herself. 'I do not want this, Mr Malone.'

The twinkle in his eye returns and he edges closer again. 'Even the way you say my name, I hear the naughtiness in your voice.'

She frowns and shakes her head. 'You're wrong, Mr Malone.'

'Why don't you call me–'

'Because you're my boyfriend's father and I will remain polite and formal with you.'

A chortle escapes his lips. 'Fine. The whole mister thing actually turns me on. I feel like I should bend you over the desk and spank you.'

Rose gasps as she witnesses a change in his gaze. His eyes are no longer enticing and sexy with a crystal glint. The shadows and dimness of the room are mirrored in his eyes as the blueness transforms into something cold and dark, almost deep black. She thinks of her boyfriend and, although he shares features with his father, she's never seen his baby-blue eyes turn this demonic shade. She longs to be in his arms, regretting ever listening to her wanton self and ending up in a locked room with his father. *How quickly the mind can change track*, she thinks.

'Mr Malone, I'm leaving now, and we will *never* be in this position again, is that clear?' Despite her attempts to remain strong, her voice falters at the end, and she can't decide if it's caused by fear or because there's a possibility, somewhere deep down, that she's lying.

'If that's truly the case, and we won't be in this position again, I'm afraid I can't let you leave.'

'W-what?' She places a hand on his chest again. This time she's powerless as he pushes against her and forces her to sit on the table.

'You've teased me one too many times... *Miss Quinn.*'

Rose's head shakes from side to side, and she wants to say no – speak the actual word – but even the smallest word can't find its way out of her dry mouth. She hears the zip of his trousers unfasten, and her skin turns ice cold as he forces his body in between her legs, places one large hand on the side of her face and the other underneath her skirt.

Chapter four

I close the living room curtains but don't move. Instead I stare at the blankness and allow the darkness to swallow me for a few moments. *BBC News* murmurs in the background; the same report repeated over and over again, new details rarely being added – just different newsreaders telling the same story – because they know it's all the city wants to hear, even if it's information they've heard a thousand times today.

It only happened this morning. A few hours ago really. Near enough the start of my shift, just another normal shift – whatever that means – although I've become accustomed to never knowing what to expect each day. But terrorism? Now the adrenaline from the day has worn off, I replay my actions in my mind, watching myself like a stranger would have done… I can't fight the pang of guilt, and the tears flow.

I saved the man who killed those Londoners. I, Abi Quinn, saved the terrorist who murdered mothers, fathers, sisters, brothers, daughters… *Oh my God, Rose!*

The tears continue to flow as I spin around in the dark room, fiddle with the lamp and search for my handbag. She must be worried sick that I haven't returned her call with everything she would have seen on TV today. How could I forget to ring her?

My damn mobile phone is nowhere to be found. Not in my bag. Not in my coat. Not in my uniform, which I packed into my rucksack before leaving the station. It was covered in blood. I still haven't had a shower. I haven't washed the awful day from my skin, and it's eight o'clock in the evening. Everything seems bigger than it is, and my head feels fit to burst.

A headache, starting small in the early morning, that builds and builds into a huge buzzing pressure against your skull, like a ball of fire, that finally explodes and sends you sliding down the wall and sitting with your head in your hands. With eyes closed, you can see yourself screaming with pain and guilt, your head thrashing from side to side. Every small inconvenience feels like the end of the world because it hurts too much. But really, on the outside, you're just sitting there, numb and looking a bit dazed. More tears fall, but they're silent and uncontrollable by this point.

Have you ever felt like that before? Have you ever had a headache that bad?

This is me right now.

I can't really be sure of the reason why. Because I can't find my phone and so desperately want to talk to Rose? Oh, to hear my daughter's voice right now... There's always such a beautiful calmness to it. Because innocent people died today, people on their way to work and school who kissed their loved ones goodbye this morning not knowing it would be for the last time? Or is it because I didn't save them? Instead I saved the man who committed that vulgar act. Perhaps I'm a monster too. Not only do I save criminals – no, terrorists – but if I can also–

'Abi.'

The voice drags me from the dangerous undercurrent of my thoughts, and I wipe the tears and snot from my face. My name is said again, shouted this time. It's coming from the front door. I grab the sofa and pull myself up, confusion clouding my mind. My legs feel unstable, unready to support me again. Pins and needles shoot from my thighs to my toes and back up again. How long was I sat down there?

'Abi, I know you're in there.' The voice is quickly recognisable. 'Come on, open up, I need to pee.'

It's Adele. Of course.

Clarity comes with a few shakes of the head and I rush to the door and open it. My co-worker and friend is stood on my

15

doorstep with a bottle of wine in one hand and a pizza box in the other. There are some people in life who just know, aren't there? They just know when you need a smile from a friendly face and an evening of indulging. Those friends – the ones who can take you away from the demons in your mind, who can make you shake away the memories of past mistakes just as those memories are about to darken your every thought, and not even realise you need them at that exact moment – are the friends you need to hold on to.

'Damn, girl, I've been banging and kicking the door for over ten minutes. I had to tell your nosey neighbour next door to mind her own every time she twitched her curtains. Busybody.'

Adele ignores my red and blotchy face and tells me to take the goodies while she nips to the toilet. She probably heard me crying. She says nothing about it, thankfully, I couldn't deal with that too right now. Those few minutes she takes to busy herself gives me just enough time to pat my cheeks dry and grab my compact from my handbag and dab my face. In all honesty, it does nothing to the inflamed red patches on my skin, but it makes me feel better on the inside, and that's a start.

Just over an hour later, with both the wine and pizza demolished, Adele has joined me on the carpet. It feels comforting, more of a girls' slumber party, and better than crying into my hands on my own. She's uplifted me with laughs and stories of when she was a teenager, because we both made a promise after she came out of the toilet not to talk about what had happened today. It's still playing on both our minds – that much is obvious, because how could it not? We both make a great show of ignoring it for each other. It makes me think that sometimes, our brains are truly amazing; the mind can be filled with disastrous images or plagued by guilt because of something you did in a former life, yet on the outside we can exhibit this put-together person who laughs and eats pizza and drinks wine with her friends.

'Your turn,' Adele says, and snaps me from my thoughts once again; she has a habit of doing that at the right time.

'My turn for what?'

'Tell me why you're a paramedic.'

I drain the last of the red from my glass, bat my hand in the air in an attempt to dismiss the conversation she wants to have. She stays silent, not having any of it, and so I answer, 'We've spoken about this before, surely.'

'No, we haven't. And so what if we have?'

She leaves the question hanging there and I get it. Sometimes it's good to remember where you've come from. To remember the decisions that you made as a teenager is to remember why you are who you are today. My mother used to say something like that.

I sigh heavily, scooch my bum around on the carpet to get comfortable again, and Adele smiles that award-winning smile, all white teeth and genuine happiness, knowing that she's won; I've been sucked into the late-night story-sharing saga she's begun.

'So, it started for me in 1983 when I broke my ankle…'

As I share it with Adele, my mind is instantly back there, in the woods behind my granny's garden, just after my fifth birthday, when I thought I could keep up with my cousin and his friends. They were tree-climbing one sunny afternoon and I wanted to join in. I opted for the tallest one I could find, with my invisible cape blowing behind me in the light June wind – proving that girls are just as courageous as boys – and I began my ascent. Sadly, I failed to consider my small hands, my lack of upper body strength and restricted leg length and somehow, I'm still not entirely sure how, but the sound of a branch snapping soon echoed in my ears. The gasps and yells for mothers and fathers to come and help swirled around me, mixing with the warm suffocating air as I landed with a painful thump on the prickly green grass sprouting from the hard ground, my cape rendered useless. The wind was knocked right out of me and I struggled to breathe which, looking back, wasn't a bad thing because it meant I didn't feel the initial pain in my ankle as the immediate shades of blue and purple took effect. The rest of that afternoon is a blur. I still don't remember the surgery or the hours or days that followed. As the morphine began to wear off, my mother explained that my awkward landing had meant that I'd fractured my right ankle in three places.

'Abigail, sweetheart, any fracture is ten times worse than a clean break – I'm sure I've heard that somewhere before, anyway – let alone three fractures,' she had said in her no-nonsense way. 'Your leg will be in a cast for at least six weeks and you'll need to use crutches. You can't put any weight on it while it heals.'

The doctors had operated and inserted a metal rod and six screws into my leg, to keep the bones together and assist them in mending themselves over time. It was the scars that surprised me, when they were finally revealed after the cast was cut away. A small one on the inside of my ankle and a long one on the outside; a thick, purple wound running high and deep along my slim, white legs. How had the surgeon managed to fit all that metal inside those small spaces? I must admit, the scars were quite ugly to look at. My cousin had said he wanted to be sick when the staples were removed – what with the puncture holes and bruised skin, my leg looked like a carcass hanging in a butcher's shop window – but it only fascinated me further.

I no longer wanted to climb trees. I did want to play doctors and nurses. If my mother or father had a hospital appointment, I always asked if I could go with them. I loved watching the way the nurses moved; they were quick, determined and stable in what, from the outside, looked like a tsunami of panic. When children fell in the playground, I was the first there to see the blood and the extent of their injuries. It's captivating to watch how people react so differently in these situations: scream, cry, panic, ignore it or act brave.

'And that's why you did what you did today.' Adele's smooth tones bring me back to the present – to my living room – and it's then I notice the blurry vision that the threat of my tears has conjured. 'Don't be so hard on yourself, Abi. You're a good person. You saved a man today with no discrimination whatsoever, not because you're a monster but because it's your *job* to do so.'

Had I called myself a monster in front of Adele? I shrug and lightly touch her hand. 'Thank you. I guess it's just easier to believe the bad stuff when you're locked in your own memories.'

Adele heaves herself to her feet and laughs. 'Girl, you need a date.' I frown while pulling myself up, slightly annoyed that she's gone to this topic again. She carries on anyway, just as I knew she would. 'Seriously, you talk about wanting to rescue people since you were the age of five, and how people interest you and all that...' She mimics me jabbering on with her hand. 'So why don't you get out there and meet some new people? Or, Jesus, just get laid and let your hair down. Actually, when was the last time you got some? The night Rose was conceived, I bet.'

She laughs a little too loud and I playfully whack her on the arm. Secretly my stomach flips at the memory of that night and my mind is dragged back to Rose. 'Come to think of it, you haven't seen my phone, have you?'

Adele scans the room. I explain I haven't got my phone, and that I can't remember seeing it since we were on shift. I so badly want to chat to Rose – it's been lovely having Adele here, but the anxiety of not returning my daughter's call has come back with a vengeance.

'Let me order this Uber and then you can use my phone to give that lovely daughter of yours a quick bell, just to reassure her the Double A Team are fine.' Adele rolls her eyes at the nickname she claims to hate, but she can't hide the smirk while tapping away at her phone.

When I finally have her mobile in my hand, I panic – I don't know Rose's number off by heart. That's shameful of a mother, isn't it?

'It's stored in my phone,' Adele says, obviously understanding the reasoning behind my hesitation. 'I'll just grab my coat.'

It goes to voicemail. I don't even get to hear Rose's voice – she hates the sound of her own voice on machines and has left the mechanical woman in place to give instructions. I'm about to hang up but have second thoughts and decide to leave a message.

It's late and I was a student once. She's either cramming for an assignment or drinking in the student union. Probably the latter. A message from me after the news today will be a welcome one, whatever time she gets it.

When I join Adele in the hallway, where she waited to give me privacy to make the call, I notice something off with her stance; there's an attitude oozing out of her, I can tell from the way she stands with her hand placed on her hip, the puckered lips and raised eyebrows.

'Why did you lie to Rose?'

I instinctively jerk my head backwards. 'When?'

'Just now, in your message. You said you're fine.' So much for giving me some privacy, hey, Adele. 'You are far from fine, girl, and it's okay to be honest about that. Lord knows we've had one hell of a shitstorm kinda day.'

My racing heart calms and I release a sigh. 'Oh, that. Right. It doesn't matter. I'm fine. Besides, it's okay to sometimes bend the truth if it means you're protecting the person you love.'

Adele relaxes her judging posture and opens the front door. 'Hmm, okay, but who's protecting you?' she says, leaning in to peck me on the cheek.

She closes the door softly behind her and, just like that, I'm left to the quiet and emptiness of my home again.

Chapter five

In my mind, today is a normal shift just like any other Saturday, except for the fact I saved a terrorist's life yesterday and had a draining debriefing about the whole event this morning. Dave insisted Adele and I go home, take a break and clear our heads before returning next week. I won't lie, I was surprised when Adele accepted his offer. Mainly because she's the joker, the smiley one who always drags others out of their dark abysses of self-doubt or worry or stress. However, and I know this from personal experience, there are some people who radiate constant sunshine and happiness on the outside but secretly, deep down where no one can see, they are battling their own storms. They are the strongest people I know. To make you feel better, they sacrifice their own fears and pain by pushing them to the back of their mind and locking them away... but we all know those secret dungeons have a way of opening the chained door eventually.

I'm pleased Adele's taking time for herself to get over what happened in London yesterday. These events affect everyone differently. The fact I'm still at work doesn't mean it hasn't touched my soul, or that I don't want to cry every time I see that murderer's face – my skin tingles as hot as blisters when I think of his limp grip around my wrist – it just means I'd be worse off at home. Alone. My only company would be thoughts and memories of yesterday: the blood, the confused faces in the crowds, the sounds of tears, loved ones' screams, machine guns and news helicopters. I love my job – it can be thrilling and addictive and rewarding – and since Rose went to university it's the only thing I have in my life. It's the reason I get out of bed every day, and although it can be full of sadness and trauma, there have certainly been times it's brought a smile to my face like no other job would have the power to. I've delivered babies, talked patients down from the ledge of suicide and heard the sigh of relief from family members when I've saved their mother, father, child or partner. Days like those bring sunshine to my world. They lighten the crushing weight of loneliness I sometimes feel, and it's worthwhile. I'm hoping for one of those days on this shift.

'Hey, Abi, didn't expect to see you here today.' Laura's suddenly standing in front of me, smiling. 'I saw Adele leave ages ago.'

I return the smile. Laura's a nice girl – and I can call her that because I think she's similar in age to my daughter – and just starting out on her paramedic's journey. She's always bright and helpful, regardless of the time, situation or mood. Like everyone else, she probably thinks I'm nuts for not going home after the debriefing.

'I prefer to keep my mind busy.'

'Oh, no, I totally get what you mean. That was a difficult Friday night,' she says, and pulls her blonde hair from the tight bun it's been wrapped up in during her shift. 'Even though the attack happened yesterday, the pubs and clubs were crawling with people last night as always.' She waves a hand, dismissing her own comments, and shakes her head, quickly realising this isn't something that needs any explanation to an old hand like me. I've worked my fair share of weekend night shifts in this city and they can be manic, to say the least. 'Anyway, I need to head off home and have a long soak and sleep the evening away,' Laura continues as she rolls her head from one side to the other, stretching the muscles in her neck – a movement I'm all too familiar with as it brings some relief to our strained bodies after a shift. 'Did you get your phone?'

'Pardon?' I ask, and in the same moment hate myself for not thinking of it sooner.

'I helped clean and restock the van last night and found a mobile in one of the door pockets. Adele said it was yours just before she left the station.'

And so the shift does begin with the buzz I need. 'Oh, Laura, you're an absolute bloody star. I realised last night I didn't have it at home and didn't even think if I'd put it in the ambulance.'

Laura, at least fifteen years my junior, frowns. 'I would have noticed the moment I stepped out of here.' She taps her trouser pocket. 'I can't do without Facebook and WhatsApp. Does that make me sound awful?'

Her bright emerald eyes look tired and the frown deepens on her tanned skin – except Laura doesn't come across as judgemental any more, this look is born out of uncertainty of her own priorities. I feel bad.

'Don't be silly. If I had more people to chat to, I'm sure I wouldn't have left it behind.' I giggle. It's fake, but has the desired effect on the younger woman, who laughs too, and then rattles on about social media being a necessary obsession in everyone's lives.

Finally, she tells me where my mobile's been left and says goodbye. I glance around, still waiting for Dave to join me – one of the boss's conditions of me finishing my shift is that I team up with him. It'll certainly be different. Anyway, he's still not here, so I leg it back to the office and hunt down my mobile phone.

How sad; Rose's two missed calls have only been joined by a notification of a voicemail, probably from my daughter too. That's all. Twenty-four hours without my phone, a terrorist attack in the city where I work and live, and no one feels the need to check in with me. But it's my own fault, I guess… distancing myself from my friends was a personal decision. Twenty-one years ago, when I finally made the choice to keep the baby growing inside me, I also made the choice that she would be my main focus in life. Followed by my work, of course, but there would be no time or space for anything or anyone else.

I can only imagine that when Adele checked her phone after we left the scene yesterday it was pinging with notifications. Text messages, missed calls, Facebook Messenger and WhatsApp messages aplenty. She's a woman surrounded by family and friends who want to know she's safe, and she deserves to be. Unlike me, Adele is a wonderful, honest person.

God! What is wrong with me? I haven't been this hard on myself since Mum went into the hospice… I have to stop.

The voicemail is from Rose, just as I predicted. Her voice is muffled and it's hard to understand what she's saying. The timestamp on the notification must be about the same time I arrived at the mosque yesterday. As the information would have already been on the news, and Rose knows my work patterns and shifts, she would have assumed that I'd be called to some part of the city to assist during the attack. Her tone doesn't sound like she's worried; it's more like she's scared. I press play to hear it again.

I definitely hear the name Dylan, and that he's found out. *Who the hell is Dylan, and what's he found out?* Rose sounds panicked. She mentions Penny too, and the pair spending time together. At least I know that one: Penny is one of her housemates in the house she shares with four other female students. Why is she talking so fast? And why is it so bloody muffled? Rather than listening to the useless message again, I decide to phone her back.

I wander towards the exit and hope Dave isn't stood by the van as I press call and wait for it to connect. The ringing sound buzzes in my ear for a nanosecond before cutting to her voicemail again. *Fuck's sake, damn voicemail!*

'Abi, category one. We're up. Come on, let's go,' Dave shouts at me as he walks towards the van, and the look on his face is one of pure impatience, as if he's been yelling at me for ages.

I have no choice but to slip the phone in my pocket and jump in the passenger seat of the ambulance. He reels off the information about our first job together and something inside me switches. I've never put Rose to the back of my thoughts, but I've learnt to move her slightly to the side of them when I'm at work. Realistically, she has her own life living away from home, enjoying university, and has been gone for nearly a year now. I have to accept that. It's difficult… a difficult feeling and a difficult emotion to describe. I mean, you want your children to grow into well-rounded adults, fend for themselves and enjoy life's experiences and adventures, of course you do, but when they leave, they take a part of you with them. A part of your heart is missing. Yes, that's a huge cliché. Damn, it's the truth; I cried every night for at least a week when Rose moved to Brighton. It's not even a million miles away, but she wasn't with me and it hurt like hell. Still does. Well, it stings. It was after she left when I understood how my parents must have felt when I packed my bags for Scotland.

A shiver snakes down my back. Scotland is something I'd rather not think about at all, although sometimes, particularly late at night when I'm alone, it's hard to think of anything but. And so, I do what I do best and push my job to the forefront of my mind, knowing it will keep me busy enough until the end of my shift. After returning to London from university, and giving birth to Rose, I knew the only way to redeem myself for what happened in Scotland was to spend my life helping others. And right now, we were on our way to see a child who was having difficulty breathing and needed my full concentration.

Chapter six

Six minutes after receiving the initial 999 call, we pull onto a road which looks more like a street preparing for Notting Hill Carnival than it does a quiet cul-de-sac estate in the heart of Belsize Park. Kids and adults are waving us down, fear etched on their faces, clamouring for our attention. As I climb down from the ambulance and grab my green response bag from the van's side cupboard, it's hard to make any sense of their cries of panic.

'This way, quickly.' A burly man pushes through the crowd blocking the pathway to the terraced house. Number sixteen – the one we need. 'It's my niece, she's stopped breathing,' he continues as he thrusts the people aside effortlessly. It's stereotypical to say all muscular bald men are bouncers, but it's exactly how he makes me feel as we're ushered into the front door with no hassle.

'Hello, paramedics are here,' Dave calls out from behind me, his voice loud and clear to announce our arrival to anyone else in the house. I simply follow the uncle on a mission in front of me and the sounds of whimpering.

It's hard to ignore the balloons and happy birthday banners, as well as the tons of sweets I'm trying not to crush into the carpet – obvious wins from the broken and beaten-up unicorn piñata on the floor. What was obviously a scene filled with laughter, celebrations, children and music just moments earlier has quickly been replaced with dread, alarm and tears.

'Please, we're in here!' A woman's screams echo through the house and the bouncer-like uncle leads us off to the left, as if he's following the trail of sweets beneath our feet.

A young woman with a stylish blonde bob is kneeling on the floor, wailing as she cradles a little girl with blonde curls stuck to her forehead, rocking her back and forth in a trembling motion. Even while my mind takes in all this information, my body reacts to the crisis in front of me like a mechanical robot. It knows what to do in an emergency, even when I feel like my brain isn't communicating the necessary actions. My response bag is on the floor and I'm trying to pry the little girl out of the woman's grasp.

'She's not breathing. S-s-she choked.' The woman stumbles over her own words and releases the girl to me.

'I'm Abi and this is Dave. What's the girl's name?'

The woman continues to cry. The uncle steps forward and lifts her off the floor, shielding her view with his broad chest, and answers my question. 'Her name's Tilly. This is her mum, my sister. Tilly's six years old. Today. This is her birthday party.'

'Tilly, can you hear me?' I call out, knowing she can't. The red flush on her cheeks and pale lips tell me everything. The family are right. The little girl isn't breathing. 'Do you know what happened?'

'I don't usually let her have sweets.' Despite the continued sobs, the mum seems to have regained some control over her sentences. 'But it's a party. The stupid piñata was my idea. How could I be so reckless?'

'No time for all that now, my love. Do you know what Tilly was eating?' Dave reads my mind – asking the question I would have – as I grab a laryngoscope from the bag, open the girl's mouth and use it to look deeper in her airway.

'I filled it with loads of different sweets. She must have grabbed one of the bigger ones – what are they called, gobstoppers? – while I wasn't looking. I called an ambulance straight away, and Mark here even clapped her on the back, but it was… it was…' The wails return, and the woman buries her face in her brother's chest again.

'It didn't work. I couldn't get it out,' Mark said. 'She was gasping for air, the poor mite, and then… just as we heard your sirens, Tilly stopped breathing completely.'

'I can see the sweet,' I calmly say while picking up the forceps to use alongside the laryngoscope – its small light aiding me also.

Dave kneels down next to me. 'It's already been a few minutes since her last breath, Abi. I think we should do a needle cric–'

'A what?' The mother spins round and hunches over me. I can feel her hot erratic exhales on the back of my neck. 'What are you going to do to my baby?'

'We may need to get front-of-neck access to Tilly. It won't get the sweet out, but the incision in her neck will allow ventilation to her lungs.'

The mother replies with a high-pitched shriek. The rest of her cries are muffled as Mark pulls his sister away from me.

Despite my explanation of the procedure, I ignore Dave's suggestion and continue to use the forceps. 'No, I've got this. I can do it.'

'Abi, there's no need for risks. We need to get her breathing.'

Dave's hovering over me. The beads of sweat building at the front of his forehead are hard to ignore. He's always had this look of Prince William about him – of a man who aged too soon, lost most of his hair and took the weight of the world on his shoulders too early in life. It occurs to me then that I have no idea how old he is. I've always assumed he's in his forties, like me. Who knows?

The look of doubt on his face is clear. Doesn't he believe I can do this? Do *I* really believe I can do this? Maybe he's right. I should just use a cannula to create a small hole in the girl's throat… but no, there's no need to do that. I lock eyes with him, steady my voice and say, 'I can get her breathing without needing access to the front of her neck, Dave.'

I sound so formal in the midst of chaos, I surprise myself – and convince myself too.

Slowly, my hand hovers over Tilly's small lips, which now have a hint of blue to them, and I pull her chin down as far as I can. My fingers flex before lowering the forceps into her mouth and throat, her reclining position assisting the movement. The sound of a clock ticking rings in my ears – I have no idea whether it's a real clock in the room that I was unaware of before, or if my mind has conjured a cruel timer that only I can hear, reminding me that every second longer I take is a second longer that this little girl's brain is starved of oxygen. Finally, the forceps clink against the hard-boiled sweet, and with swift automatic movements I use the pincers to pull the obstruction from Tilly's airway.

'Dave, pass me the bag and mask.'

My partner is ready and waiting, and we swap equipment seamlessly.

'What's happening?' Mark calls from behind me.

'Abi managed to reach the sweet, but Tilly is hypoxic–'

'What?' the mother cries.

'Tilly is lacking oxygen, so Abi is using the bag valve mask which is connected to the oxygen to help her breathe.' I can hear the calmness in Dave's voice.

'Oh, baby girl, come on. Breathe for Mummy. Come on, birthday girl. Come on…'

Drowning out the mother's voice, which feels very close to my ear again, I continue to give Tilly five rescue breaths. Just as I count the last one, the little girl groans under the mask.

I breathe myself – one slow, deep exhale – before requesting Dave returns to the ambulance so he can radio ahead to The Royal Free Hospital.

'Tills, baby, can you hear me? It's Mummy.'

I hold the mother back from the child slightly. 'Please, we still need to give Tilly some space. She's coming around but she's going to be very groggy and confused because of the hypoxia. We can't be sure how this affected her body. Just give her some time.'

'W-w-what–' Tilly's soft voice is cut off by the roughness of her throat.

'Don't try to speak, Tilly,' I whisper softly. 'You're safe and your mummy and Uncle Mark are here with you. Don't you worry.'

The woman throws her arms around my neck and I have to use my free hand to balance on the floor, so we both don't topple backwards.

'Thank you so much, Abi. Thank you, thank you, thank you,' she whispers in my ear.

Dave's back in the room, and when the woman finally lets me go, I smile. 'And you are?'

She frowns. 'I'm Tilly's mum.'

'I meant your name.'

She smiles for the first time. 'Dee. Dee Williams.'

'Well, Ms Williams, we need to take Tilly to the hospital straight way. You're more than welcome to ride along with us.'

The tears return and gush silently down Dee's face. She shakes her head as Dave and I transfer the weak little girl from the floor to the stretcher. 'I don't know how you do it. I could never have done what you just did right in front of us. And thank you for not cutting my baby's neck open. You're a hero. No, not just any old hero, you're *my* hero. You saved my little girl and she means the world to me.'

Once outside, greeted by cheers and applause from the relieved family members and friends, I ask Dave to ride in the back with the Williams. It's only a short journey to the hospital, but I need to be alone, get my heart beating at a normal speed again. My hands didn't shake once while I held the forceps in little Tilly's mouth. Now they're gripped around the steering wheel so tightly that my knuckles are pure white because... well, because I'm so afraid that if I let go, they'll shake so much that they'll never stop.

It's an honour to be called a hero, of course it is, yet I never feel like one because this is my *job*. I'm here to save that small child and anyone else who calls 999, and while it's not an easy thing to do, the thought of that little girl lying in her living room – during her own birthday party – not making it... that's what makes me do it. Not every patient is saved, sadly. It does happen, lives are lost. It's happened to me and most paramedics I know, and we certainly don't feel like heroes on those days – we're not called heroes on those days, either. So perhaps I should take it when I can. Take the hugs and kind words from the mums and dads and all the family members, because I gave them that happiness, and in that moment in their lives, I am their hero.

I sniff back the threatening tears, the overspill of emotion that I had to keep hold of while I was in that house, the overwhelming feeling I had to burst into tears when I heard Tilly inhale the stuffy air surrounding us. The aftermath of a job is intense, but my God it's easier than losing a patient. Knowing that six-year-old girl is safe in the back of my ambulance with Dave and her mum should bring a smile to my face, and so I let it. I know Tilly and Dee have stamped themselves on my memory – their cries and wails and questions of confusion, their small voices and innocent faces – and I won't be forgetting the mother and daughter any time soon.

* * *

After what seems like hours since we left the Williams home, we're finally ready to sign off from the job – now that Tilly and mum Dee are settled in at the hospital. Dave and I took some time in the canteen to grab a bite to eat and fill out our report, but he's gone off somewhere and I'm left waiting for him once again. Standing alone at the entrance of the A&E, I tuck myself behind the van where no one can see me and wait to return to the station. In a world so hectic and full of people – a lot of them wanting your attention, especially when you're in uniform and looking idle at a hospital – it's nice to just step back for a minute and watch it all move around you. To go unnoticed can be a good thing, sometimes.

The hectic day has disappeared behind a cloak of quiet darkness, and the large moon dominates the black, starless sky. My mum had a saying about this, that the crazies came out with a full moon. I'd sigh, explaining her use of language to describe these criminals was offensive and inaccurate, but she was old school and refused to change; her inappropriateness has only magnified since living at the hospice. I also wanted her to understand that I've worked many jobs – day and night, full moon, half-moon and no moon – and there are plenty of delinquents out there. The lunar cycle, the weather, the time of the year doesn't seem to make a difference. I think if something's destined to happen, it'll happen, and there's nothing any of us can do about it. We've all got our quirky ways of thinking to get us through life, I guess.

Something Dee said to me earlier rings in my ears like the siren from my ambulance: *You saved my little girl and she means the world to me.* My heart hurts and I've never wanted to be hugged so badly. By my own mum… and by Rose.

I grab my phone and ring my daughter's number. There's a few seconds of ringing before the voicemail kicks in and greets me again. My hand shakes, and I feel the mobile tremble in my fingers as my frustration morphs into fear. Clicking on the WhatsApp icon, I pull up Rose's profile – the picture shows her gorgeous smiling face, big red lips and poker-straight black hair – and wait for the device to tell me when she was last seen online. Yesterday afternoon. Before she left the voicemail on my phone.

The wind is knocked right out of me as I slide down the side of the ambulance. You just know – as a parent that is – you just know these things, and this is not a good sign. It's been two full days since I've heard my daughter's voice, and while I know that isn't extreme, the fact that she hasn't been on WhatsApp for well over twenty-four hours is unheard of.

Deep breaths, Abi. Slowly in and out.

She's a grown woman, for crying out loud, so what if she hasn't been on her phone?

But when is Rose without her phone? It would need to be surgically removed from her hand.

Perhaps it's broken, drunkenly dropped down the loo at some party.

But then she would have contacted me another way.

This is trivial. So what if she hasn't been on WhatsApp?

But it's how I've always checked in on her. It's how I know she's okay. Rose is always on some form of social media.

'Jesus, Abi, are you that dog-tired you need to wait for me on the ground?' Dave says with a laugh. His face turns serious when I look up at him. 'Shit, what's wrong?'

'I haven't spoken to Rose for two days and her phone keeps going to voicemail,' I blurt out, and it feels pathetic saying it aloud, especially from my crumbling position down here, but I continue anyway, 'You'll think I'm nuts, Dave. But we're more than just mother and daughter, we're best friends, and I've never gone this long without speaking to her. With everything that happened in the city yesterday, she would have wanted to check I'm okay. It would have been all over the news and–'

'Whoa, calm down,' he interrupts me, and hands me a packet of pocket tissues from his jacket. He says nothing, just waits for me to sort myself out, then puts his hand out. 'Come on, I'm not joining you on the ground. My back hates me enough as it is from carting these patients back and forth.'

His smile is infectious, and I can't help returning one, as slight as it may be, while taking his hand and letting him pull me up. Dave places a large palm on each of my cheeks and his touch causes an electric shock to pass between us. He stays firm; his blue eyes bore into mine.

'It doesn't sound stupid that the two of you are best friends. My mum and sister were exactly the same.'

'You don't understand, Dave. We've never had a big family like yours. It's me and Rose, just the two of us. That's how it's always been. We've been through so much...' I stop myself.

He releases my face and steps back. He's nodding, as if he agrees and understands, but I can tell he's about to argue against what I'm feeling.

'Abi, you're overreacting. I have no doubt how close the two of you are... but she's caught up in one of life's biggest rites of passage. It's *university*, for heaven's sake. Rose is busy doing things she doesn't want her mum to know about. I mean, come on, you have to understand that. You took off completely; Scotland, wasn't it?'

I flinch. 'How do you know that's where I went to uni?'

He frowns, but his smile stays in place as he shrugs. 'Dunno. Adele probably mentioned it to me. My point is, as much as Rose is your best friend – and you hers – she is meeting new people and it's one big funfair in your first year.'

I try to let Dave's sensible words wash over me, convince me that I *am* overreacting and he's completely right. But I can't shake the memory of *my* first year at university, and the people I met, and that's exactly what leads me back to panic.

'Look, why don't we go for a drink, take your mind off everything?'

He's sweet and charming, and with his remaining wispy hair and pearly white smile, he really does look like a prince right now. I've never wanted a knight in shining armour – or a prince for that matter – to save me. If I had, my life might be completely different today.

'Thanks, Dave, but no. Not tonight, anyway. I just want to get home.'

'Fair dos. You know where I am if you change your mind. Jump in, I'll drive us back,' he says, and vanishes into the ambulance.

Involuntarily, my chest jerks and I heave. I have no control over the retching motion and the bile escaping my mouth. I spit it on the ground, use the tissue to dry my lips and chin and walk round to the passenger door of the van. Regardless of Dave's calming words, my mind feels numb, with one question spinning in circles around it: why can't I get in contact with Rose?

Chapter seven

I'm home. Not quite sure how I got here – on autopilot, perhaps – but here I am, still wearing my coat. No lights are on in the house, and I'm sat on the sofa with my phone in my hand. I've checked them all, all the different ways Rose and I communicate: Facebook, Snapchat, WhatsApp, Instagram. They're not only the methods we use, but they are her links to the world too; like most people nowadays.

Yet Rose hasn't posted one picture, been tagged in one status or sent one message. Why? I'm really trying not to overreact – trying to put Dave's sensible words on repeat and not let my brain go to the most awful places, but I can't help it. I've seen teenagers and young people on the streets, alone and afraid in London because they've lost their friends, they've been mugged or beaten up – both, more often than not – or they've been knocked down by a speeding car. Sometimes, it's not their home town and they're dazed or confused and don't know what to do. Just like Brighton isn't Rose's home town – a town as busy and bustling as London.

But she has her uni friends, her housemates, and they wouldn't abandon her, would they?

My fingers dance across the screen of my phone. They have no purpose. They don't know which app to select. I'm instructing my digits to contact her friends, press call on their numbers, until I realise I don't have their contact details. Can that be true? Have I really never asked Rose for an emergency contact number? A friend's or a housemate's? I have numbers for her school friends – hell, I even know where some of them live – but none of them went to Brighton University, so what would be the point? Surely she wouldn't be in contact with one of them before trying to call me again?

It's Rose's first year of university. How could I not have asked for contact numbers? My panic turns to anger, the darkness of the room enveloping my mood while I grow madder and madder at myself. When she had chosen to rent a large house with four strangers rather than apply for halls of residence on campus, I'd been a bit dubious. As always, Rose talked me round to her way of thinking – it was still close to uni, but it was cheaper, and she wouldn't have to house search again during her course. Wouldn't that have been my cue to run a check on who she was actually living with? If she had chosen to live in halls, if I had fought a bit harder against her decision, I could probably ring the campus now and check in on her.

Really, Abi? Because yes, there's someone employed by Brighton University to work on campus and shield calls from worried parents up and down the country – overseas probably have their own dedicated hotline, of course – and personally visit each hall of residence to check said child is alive and well and not comatose in a pool of their own hung-over vomit.

What the fuck is wrong with me?

I need to get out of my own head before I send myself insane. *Okay, it's a Saturday evening and I'm off rota now for two days. Get your sensible cap on, Abi.*

I switch on the lamp, shed my coat and boots and decide to run a warm bath. The last forty-eight hours have been manic and I'm not thinking straight. While the water's running, I'll check the train times to Brighton tomorrow morning and just head up there. Rose is not in any danger. She's being a forgetful free-spirited student in her first year of uni, and I'm just a cool mum on a surprise visit on my day off.

Sorted.

Except my foot isn't even on the first stair and the landline rings. My entire body is attacked with a voltage of nerves that makes me run to the phone without even thinking. My hand shudders as I reach for it. It can only be bad news. Who calls landlines any more? I only have it because it came as a package deal with the Internet.

'Hello,' I croak and quickly clear my throat.

'Can I speak to Ms Quinn please?'

Oh, sweet Jesus. Please be PPI, please be PPI. Don't be a hospital. Don't be a hospital.

'Speaking.'

'This is Trudy from the hospice—'

'Oh my God, I knew it. What's wrong with her?'

'Now please, Ms Quinn, there's no reason to panic—'

'Where is she? Which hospital?'

The woman trips over her words and I want to punch her like I've never wanted to punch anyone in my life. 'Er… Ms Quinn, I'm calling from Baytree Hospice regarding your mother. It's Trudy, the night nurse. I think we've only met the once.'

My breath catches in my throat and a weird gurgling noise escapes my mouth. I wipe the silent tears that have started to fall and try to pull myself together.

'Ms Quinn, are you okay? Please don't panic. Your mum is okay, but she hasn't had a great day is all. She's called for you quite a few times today, and the day staff didn't feel it warranted a phone call to you. These things are regular occurrences here, as I'm sure you understand.'

'S-s-so… w-w-w…' I take another moment. 'I'm sorry, Trudy. What's made you call me now?'

The woman on the other end practically whispers, like she doesn't want those around her to hear some secret she's telling me. 'Ms Quinn, I'm quite a fan of your mother and I just wanted you to be aware of the situation really. I'm sorry, perhaps it's inappropriate. But I just know she'll have a better night's sleep if she sees you first. Gets to say goodnight. It's hardly fair not to when she's been asking for you all day. I know you work on a shift pattern and it's not always easy for you—'

'Trudy, say no more, I'm leaving my house this second. Tell my mum I'm on my way and I shouldn't be more than half an hour.'

I hang up, grab my bag and coat from the sofa, slip my feet back into my boots while switching the lamp off and head for the front door. It doesn't change my plans for tomorrow, and I can check the train times to Brighton later. Mum might actually be able to talk some sense into me.

I can't help chuckling at my own naivety as I jump in the car.

* * *

The drive from my home in East Finchley to the hospice in Aldenham takes almost half an hour, thanks to the traffic on the M1. I never wanted my mother to be so far from me, but Baytree is such a beautiful building surrounded by golf courses and country clubs, farms and heaths – and I wanted Mum to have stunning scenery. Beats the built-up-and-busy view she had from the dining-room-cum-bedroom we made in her Wembley home after my father passed away. The area grew in popularity with football and NFL games being played at the iconic stadium, and it could sometimes take me longer to get to her when she lived there. Aldenham wasn't just a pretty move, it was a smart one too, though I'm sure she doesn't feel like that today, when she's been calling out for me all day.

Thank God for Trudy, and for her getting in touch with me.

I breeze through the security measures in place at Baytree, despite this not being my regular time to visit. Most of the staff know me. Or maybe it's because I didn't have time to change out of my uniform and they've just assumed another poor soul has pegged it and I'm here to escort the body from the premises. It sounds like we – emergency service professionals, carers – are a cold-hearted bunch. We're not; we're just used to death. We've become accustomed to it. Old, young, sick or healthy, the grim reaper really doesn't discriminate – and we've seen it all.

The screech from my mother's room makes me run down the hallway; whether Trudy was lying or not earlier, things sound far from fine now. At the doorway to her room I stop and wait. I don't know why, but I can't go in. Like a vampire who needs permission, I'm stuck here, just watching and waiting.

Two male nurses are trying to pin my mother to the bed, and a female nurse, who I assume is Trudy, is gently trying to cajole her. It isn't working. There's no aggression, and the men don't seem to be using brute force, but it's the wildness of my mother that's stopped me in my tracks. Her usually tidy white hair is unruly and unkempt, standing on end, to the point where she looks like Albert Einstein, minus the tash, thankfully. She's so thin… with her petite body, her bony hands and her wrinkled flustered face. My mother's floral nightie has ridden up to her knees as she's thrashed about trying to get out of the bed, and I step forward, without thinking, and pull the hem of it back down to her ankles.

There's a wave of silence in the room as my mother stops fighting against the nurses and reaches out to stroke my hair. Her long slender fingers, like those of a pianist, find their way to my earlobe and she rubs it. She told me I used to do this to her when I was a child; it had been *my* way of finding calm and falling asleep.

'Abigail,' she whispers, and everything changes. Just like that.

The male nurses tuck my mother into bed now that she has let go of my ear. Her eyes never move from me, and Trudy promises that this *episode* – as they like to call it – had only started five minutes ago. I believe her, I think. I still ask her to leave me and my mother alone.

'Kitty, I'm going to leave you with Abi now.'

My mother dismisses the nurses with a flick of her hand, a frown line deeply burrowed in her forehead. I know that frown – it's one of annoyance, not confusion. She wants them gone as much as I do. I love it when my mother's like this: in control of her feelings. With it – rational and lucid, I mean.

There are days when I visit and I could be here an hour before she recognises who I am. I talk about my childhood, her bingo outings, about Dad, about her working as a caregiver for most of her life – helping people who were in the same situation she is in now. Actually, perhaps that's something she doesn't want to remember. But nothing seems to register. Mum's been in this hospice for five years. Five. Sometimes that feels like a lifetime in itself, probably because I just never know which Kitty I'm going to interact with when I get here: the confused young girl who doesn't have a daughter, the frustrated adult who thinks I'm still a teenager, or Kitty my mother who remembers everything. Too much, sometimes.

From the smile on her face, tonight is a good night, despite the *episode* I was greeted with, because she knows who I am. I join her on the bed, my bum half on and half off because I don't want to ask her to move now that she seems so comfortable. There's a brush on the bedside table, calling out to be used, and I snatch it up and get to work on taming my mother's hair. She would hate to see herself like this; Mum is a woman who, while never overdone with make-up, always took pride in her appearance. I should say *takes* pride… she's not dead yet. Just allowing that thought to enter my head for the briefest of moments causes a rogue tear to leak from my eye. Anyway, her hair was always a major part of who she was – always dyed with that one same black colour whenever she spied a streak of white, and always set in curlers to give it a natural-looking bounce. Mum would hate to see herself like this, even more so when there were strangers in the room, so I take my time stroking the brush from root to tip until it's tidy enough to wrap up in a high and neat chignon bun. She likes that hairstyle, or at least she used to.

As I return the hairbrush to its home on the nightstand, my mum reaches a hand up to rest it on my face. I place my own hand over hers, can feel the slight shake to her unsteady touch, can trace the lines of wrinkles and veins under my own finger, but her skin still feels as soft as ever. She still feels like Mum.

'Abigail?' she whispers again, this time in a tone that makes me feel like she's reassuring herself that it's really me.

It's dementia, by the way, if you hadn't already guessed. And although Mum's lived here for five years, she's probably suffered with the disease for quite a while – at least seven years, I'd estimate. It was just easier to ignore – that's the wrong word – it was easier to deny when my father was alive. He took care of Mum, and I think he hid quite a lot from me. Undoubtedly, he assumed he could handle things, that she would leave this world before him, so he didn't need to worry me. Funny how life really can change in the blink of an eye. The fearful C-word. There's quite a few of those, isn't there? Christmas. Cunt. Chlamydia. But no, it was the real dreaded C-word that no one wants to hear, yet so many people do on a daily basis. Cancer. Dad didn't even have a chance to battle against it. Diagnosis to funeral in four months.

I still haven't decided which is crueller: losing your hero suddenly without having the chance to say all the things you wanted and needed to – namely how sorry you were for disappointing them – or watching the woman who raised you crumble away in front of your eyes, losing a small piece of her every single day. Can one actually be worse than the other?

'Abigail, what are you thinking about?' Mum's voice is still soft, but not so much of a murmur as it was before. Her strength rebuilds the calmer she is after an episode.

I use the break in silence to get off the bed, pull the armchair closer to my mother and sit down. I grab her hand again, squeeze it a bit tighter and smile. 'I was thinking about Dad.'

'Ah, that man fills my thoughts most hours. From when we were teenagers waltzing around the dance halls, to having you – our only child – and then becoming grandparents to our little flower.'

I feel the lump in my throat gather momentum and it takes me a while to force it down. 'A lot of lovely memories, Mum.'

'How is the baby?'

My tearful emotions are replaced by a sad sigh. 'Rose isn't a baby any more, Mum. She's a grown woman, remember? Studying at Brighton University. Oh, you were so proud of her when she told you she'd been accepted.'

I think of how much I want to be on a train heading to the seaside town right now; I'm so desperate to see my daughter. Mum distracts me again. There's a change in her expression, a change to her frown, and I wonder if I'm about to lose her.

'And Patrick, how is he?'

Crap. 'Mum, please can we not do this?'

'You need to tell that man about the baby.'

I release her hand and fidget with my own fingers, unable – unwilling – to look at her. 'Patrick died, Mum. You know that.'

'Stop lying, Abigail Quinn.'

My head snaps up; something in my mother's voice is different. There's definitely no more weakness in her body. She looks like my mother from ten, twelve, twenty years ago. A look of fury in her eyes and life in her cheeks again. For the first time in a long time I see the woman my mother used to be.

'Patrick never died, Abi, stop lying. If I told you once, I've told you a million times: the truth will always out.'

I move back from the bed, almost as if she'd pushed me away with her words. Mum hasn't spoken to me like that since Rose was a baby, when she agreed to keep my secret. It was for the best. It was for Rose.

'You can't play with people's lives, Abi. You've lied to that girl for twenty years. And what about Patrick? Don't you think he has a right to know?'

She's wagging her finger like an angry headmistress – and I feel like a naughty schoolgirl. I get up and walk to the end of the bed, grip the iron bar at the base of it and stumble over my own words. It's been so long since she's confronted me about it, I'm truly at a loss for words.

'M-mum, what do you mean? Patrick died, remember?'

As quick as she returned, my mum is gone; the flustered cheeks give way to a grey tinge and she's poking her temple rather than pointing at me. 'Yes, I remember now, Abigail. I'm sorry.'

Mum is lost and confused, and I put her there. The guilt pushes me back to her and I scoop her up in a hug. Her frail body crushes against me and I feel her ribs under my hands.

'I'm so sorry Patrick died. How sad for you and Rose.'

My chest feels like it's trying to crush my heart, the pressure getting tighter and tighter as I hold back the tears. It's one thing lying to my daughter – she knows no different – but my mother knows the truth and I've sent her mind to purgatory to keep my evil secret safe.

But is it safe? That's the first time since Mum's been in this hospice that she's challenged me about Patrick. What if more memories return the next time Rose is here? She'll question me... I'll need to be prepared.

What if I'm not here when Rose visits?

Panic claws up my throat like a savage and trapped beast, and the urge to find my daughter becomes even more paramount.

Chapter eight

I'm late. Fucking stupidly late, and I hate myself for it. I had such enthusiastic plans to be up early this morning – not as early as the first train from Victoria to Brighton at something absurd like 5am; Rose would definitely click-on to something being wrong if I rocked up to her house at six thirty in the morning. But I had plans nonetheless to be bright and energic today, painting the picture of a mother with a day off from work, taking a trip to the seaside, excited to see her daughter. However, thanks to Mum, I hardly slept at all last night.

It's the not knowing. Not knowing what my mum could say at any given time. She's the only one who shares the real secret with me and I've never worried about her slipping up before. Pathetic of me really, considering she's suffering from a disease that has slowly been damaging her brain, all her memories. How could I never think this could be a possibility? If she told Rose the truth… No, I can't even go there.

Besides, Rose still hasn't been on social media. Her phone is now going straight to voicemail without ringing and despite trying to be calm about her not calling me, every time I closed my eyes last night, I saw her petite body lying in a dark ditch. Funny how that's where our thoughts go when we think of our kids in danger: a dark trench by the side of the road, them covered in dirt and mud and calling out to us with no avail. I blame the movies. Or maybe my job. Sadly, I've witnessed these scenarios first-hand.

Sleep won at some point in the early hours. It was a sweaty and disturbed slumber and I obviously turned off my alarm instead of snoozing it. Which leads to the reason I'm running late and why I missed the earlier trains. Now I'm flustered and red from a rushed, steaming-hot shower.

Breathe, Abi.

I hate talking to myself in the mirror, but sometimes a good lecture from yourself is actually just what you need. I wipe the condensation from the glass and take a long hard look at myself. Rose looks a lot like me. I couldn't see it when she was growing up, though my parents could, thank God. I can now. Now she's an adult and has filled out and fitted into her skin, I can see the woman she is. The same features looking back at me are the same ones Rose has inherited: long dark hair, pale white skin dotted with the odd freckle here and there, deep brown eyes. It's no wonder strangers mistake us for sisters.

Despite my flustered hue, I'm still pale; the palest I've looked in years. Probably because I haven't been on a sunny break since Rose was fifteen. It was our last mother-and-daughter holiday to Spain – we visited the same place every year. That year, however, while we were sitting by the pool, Rose said she thought it best we didn't go any more, confessing that the kids at school had laughed at her when she told them. Apparently, fifteen-year-olds don't holiday with their parents any longer. Of course I was hurt; it was like a punch to the gut. I looked forward to our annual holiday during the year, but breaking away from the annual holiday with Mum is a rite of passage for any teenager and I had to accept that. Even though we didn't go to Spain again, every now and then she allowed me to take her on a shopping trip or on a day out to Southend-on-Sea. It never mattered to me where we were. As long as I got to spend quality time with my daughter, I was happy.

I exhale deeply, fogging up the mirror again, but not before noticing the look of fear etched on my face. Not only do I see it, I feel it. It's a bad case of the butterflies you don't want. These aren't the excited flutters, these are the downright terrified whacks against your insides.

My thoughts are a mix of Mum and Rose and I hate that I can't settle on one problem at a time. Although, what my mum may or may not say doesn't really matter at all if I can't find Rose. It's Sunday. I haven't spoken to her since Thursday and there's been no word from her since Friday afternoon.

That's what today is all about.

Breathe, Abi. Breathe. There's no point heading down to Brighton like this: flustered and irrational. *Push the worries aside, take one thing at a time and calm the fuck down.*

I listen to my internal self, inhaling and exhaling like a pregnant woman in early labour.

Dry yourself. Blow-dry your hair. Choose an outfit. Oh, and slap some bloody make-up on because you look like a flaming ghost. Then go from there.

And so, I focus on these initial tasks, even putting the radio on and letting some eighties classics flow through my body as I prance around my bedroom. It can only be a good day if you let it be one, and that's exactly what today will be.

* * *

An hour later, I'm dressed and have painted a new woman on my face – well, a fresh woman with some bronzer and pink lip gloss. I've had breakfast and googled the later trains from London Victoria to Brighton. It's a very short walk from my house to East Finchley Underground Station, and two trains will get me into Victoria in twenty-four minutes. I'll have time to buy a ticket for the 10.25am train and will arrive at the seaside for 11.31am. Then, when I get to Rose's house and we've had a cuddle and laugh at my expense, I can offer to buy her lunch.

Sorted.

The doorbell sounds just as I reach it to open it and leave. Adele is standing there, a huge smile plastered across her beautiful brown skin. I'm sure she's never visited my home so much in the past. Shit, I can tell by her face she wants to come in.

Of course, things aren't as sorted as I tried to believe. Is anything ever simple?

I don't mean to sound rude, but I can't help it. I have to stick with my plan today. I can't be sidetracked again. This is too important.

'Adele, I'm really sorry, love. I was just heading out.'

'Oh,' she says, and drums her hands against the top of her thighs like someone lost. I feel bad. 'I thought we could grab some breakfast together.'

'Why didn't you call?'

'I rushed out of work so quickly, I didn't know if you had managed to get your phone from lost property.' Her smile fades and she waves a hand as if she's being silly. 'You're right, it was silly of me to come around unannounced… again. I'm sorry.'

I glance at my watch, annoyed, but offer her a smile. 'Don't be sorry. It's just that I thought I'd head down to Brighton today and surprise Rose.'

Adele's smile returns. 'You managed to get in touch with her then?'

'Well… no. That's why I'm surprising her.' Adele doesn't look convinced; actually, I don't know what she looks like. She doesn't look like the bright and bubbly colleague I usually share the ambulance with. 'Are you sure everything's okay?'

'Of course. I'm sorry to have bothered you, Abs. I'll head home and see you on the next shift.'

As she turns to walk away, something inside of me lurches, and I feel guilty for letting her go. Why, I don't know, but I call out, 'Adele, why don't you come with me?'

She spins around, the joy evident in her hazel eyes. 'Really? I wouldn't be intruding?'

What am I doing? 'Of course not. It'll be good to have someone on the journey with me. And I'm sure Rose would love to see you too; you guys haven't seen each other since…'

'That leaving BBQ thing you threw for her in the summer before she packed off to uni.'

'Exactly. Gosh, that seems like a lifetime ago. Is that really the last time you saw Rose?'

Adele shrugs and turns down her mouth. 'It must be. I can't think of when I would have last spoken to her.'

As I move to grab the door keys from the side cabinet, something comes back to my mind out of the blue. I turn to Adele. 'Hey, I meant to ask you, actually. Why do you have Rose's number?'

She stares at me and puckers her lips, saying nothing.

'When you came around to mine. After our job at the TA and I didn't have my phone. Rose's number was stored in your mobile.'

I must have jogged her memory enough because she makes that 'ah ha' sound, like you see the old detectives on TV do when they've solved their mystery. 'It was at that same BBQ. We exchanged numbers, for no reason really. I think it was more of a "oh, you're leaving, let's keep in touch" kinda thing. We never actually did.'

'Ha, yeah, that's always the way, isn't it? Anyway, about today. If you're free–'

'Hell yeah I am, girl. Let's have a day out by the sea.'

As I pull the front door closed, and then double lock it, Adele swoops her arm through mine and we walk, interlocked, away from my home. It's definitely not the day I planned but, for some reason, it feels nice not to be alone.

Chapter nine

As the train pulls away from London Victoria, my mood hitches up another notch and the smile on my face is involuntary; in about an hour and a half, I'll see Rose. I'll hold my daughter so tight she'll think I have flipped out.

I already brought Adele up to speed, explaining how I've felt having no contact with Rose, and her words were similar to Dave's, but not miles away from my thinking. Adele has children of her own and although they're older and have blessed her with grandchildren – and no, you would never guess Adele was a granny – she can understand the unreasonable panic when you can't get through to them. Her understanding nature has helped keep the calmness overriding the threatening storm of emotions.

'Can I be honest with you, Abi?'

Uh oh. 'Okay.'

'The real reason I came round this morning was because I've been a bit worried about you.'

My smile evaporates and I frown, surprised. That's annoying. I wanted to stay on a high. 'You have? But why?'

Adele sighs and squirms a little in her seat. 'Well, Dave called me last night – I think he'd had a few drinks, if I'm honest. He was worried about you, and how you feel about Rose... so I knew all this before you even told me. I'm sorry I didn't say anything just now. I thought it was probably good for you to get your feelings out.'

I want to be angry, but how can I be? I don't have many friends, and my family is practically non-existent, so if my work colleagues care so much about me that they're speaking to each other outside of the station, that can't be so bad, right?

'So, I thought I'd come round and take you out for breakfast – that part was true,' she continues with a smile, 'and maybe it would help you take your mind off Rose.'

My shoulders slump. 'I don't want to take my mind off–'

Adele's palm, inches from my face, cuts me off. 'I know you don't. That's why I was glad you said you were coming to Brighton this morning. You're being proactive, getting out there and doing something. I mean, not the something I've been telling you to get out there and do for ages, but nonetheless, you're being ballsy and decisive. And I like this side to Abi.'

I roll my eyes and shake my head; this woman can be impossible. Honestly, apart from Rose, she's probably my best friend. My lips tug upwards and the smile – along with the happy mood – quickly returns.

'Well, thanks for caring about me… no matter how strange it is sometimes.'

Adele laughs while cracking the ring pull of her Diet Coke. 'So, what's the plan? Do you think Rose will be at home?'

'Yeah, I would guess so. It's late Sunday morning by time the train pulls into Brighton, right? I doubt she'll be in the library.'

'Damn straight. She's probably in bed nursing a hangover if she's anything like me in my pre-grandma, pre-kids, pre-responsibility days. Oh, to be young and free and enjoy all-day drinking from Saturday afternoon to Saturday night again, and then wasting your entire Sunday recuperating and feeling sorry for yourself, of course.'

'What, like that man we were called to at The Grand Junction pub? Sprawled out by the canal, baking in the sun and choking on his own vomit?' I quickly remind her. 'Enough to put you off drinking fruity cider in the sunshine for a lifetime.'

She pulls a face as the train stops at Burgess Hill; just two more stops and we're there. The butterflies have stayed with me, though they're no longer abusing me from the inside; I feel their wings like a graceful dance. It's welcome… it's nice. There's also a sneaky glimmer of heat from the weak sun building strength in the distance and peering in through the train window. That's welcome too, because it fits just perfectly with the jovial mood this morning.

The quietness of the carriage is disrupted by a group of girls getting on the train. I say group, but when I peer around to where they've sat behind us, I'm shocked to find there's only three of them. They're making enough noise that you'd be forgiven for thinking that a hen party had just joined the 10.25am train to Brighton. Usually, the disturbance would irk me slightly. I mean, I'm no old fuddy-duddy, but I hate the way some people – and I'm not saying it's always young people – think that public transport belongs to them solely. That they can cackle and scream and speak at a decibel so loud the entire train can hear them. Come on, the world doesn't revolve around you.

And just as quickly as the thought comes, I feel guilty. I must remember I was their age once: excited, carefree and just enjoying life. They mean no harm. Not like I did when I was their age–

'What do you think?' Adele's waving her hand in my face; I go cross-eyed trying to focus.

'About what?'

'I'd say those girls are from Brighton Uni. They're talking about a pub quiz happening this afternoon.'

'Hardly conclusive evidence.'

Adele pouts and makes a weird humming noise through her lips. 'No, maybe not. What about the Brighton University jumper that one of them is wearing?'

I quickly gaze over my shoulder again, surprised I missed it the first time. Turning back to Adele, it's hard to ignore her raised eyebrows and smirk. 'Alright, alright, fair game, guv,' I say, and hold my hands up in mock surrender to her smugness.

She's off her seat in one swift movement and joins the students. Her presence doesn't dull their enthusiasm; in fact, it seems to only encourage it more as they go full throttle into the details about the weekly pub quiz at the university's student union. I think I remember Rose mentioning it before. I can't be entirely sure.

They continue to explain that it's a great way to get the students who have buggered off for the weekend back to campus, in time for lectures on Monday, because they offer a happy hour, cheap booze and decent prizes. The trio don't live far, but they always make sure they're back for the quiz, like most of the students, apparently. It's very popular, so they tell Adele. When they've told her all she wants to know, Adele's back in her seat with an aura of giddiness about her.

'I think they've rubbed off on you.'

'Their zest for fun is infectious, I'll admit.' She laughs. 'But it definitely sounds like it's the place to head straight to. The quiz starts at half past twelve; the girls say everyone's there about an hour before to get a seat and register their team.'

I hesitate. That wasn't the plan. Meet Rose at her house and go for lunch. That was the plan.

As if Adele's read my mind, she rolls her eyes. 'Look, there was no plan and Rose doesn't know you're coming. If this quiz is as popular as those girls say, then surely Rose and her housemates go every Sunday.'

'I thought you said Rose would be hungover in bed like you would have been,' I reply with a smirk of my own.

'Ah, but you're forgetting about the hair of the dog.'

I can't help but laugh. 'We can actually walk the route to Rose's house which takes us past the student union first.'

'There you go. Your plan hasn't really been disrupted, in that case. A small detour is all.'

She has a point. I'm not completely sold on it but it wouldn't hurt to cover all the bases. 'Why do I feel you're more excited about entering a student union, a place filled with young men and booze?'

Adele gasps. 'Abigail Quinn. What are you implying? I'm a happily married woman. A mother and a grandmother. I'm just here for a day out with my friend, to have lunch with her and her daughter.'

She's trying to make light of the situation, and I'm really trying to ignore the panic gripping me. I can't keep up with my own bloody emotions. We don't know if Rose will be at the student union, or if she'll be at home nursing a hangover, or if she even fucking cares about the stupid pub quiz. That's the whole point: I don't know where my daughter is. Suddenly, the bright and breezy Abi of an hour ago is kicked out of the pilot's seat and I'm left an angry, confused woman grinding her jaw shut in fear of shouting out her worst nightmares.

I gaze out the window, ignoring Adele as she continues to witter on about God knows what, and watch the sun disappear behind the greyest of clouds. The sliver of hope that the sunshine would grace our day at the seaside is over. There's no coming back from that brimming dark sky, tempting a downpour to wash away any optimism I had.

If needs be, I'll leave Adele at the student union with her new girlie friends and head off to find Rose myself. I should have listened to my own damn gut. Going this long – this many days and hours and minutes – without hearing from Rose is unheard of. Add that to the fact that there's been no social media activity on Rose's part… well, that's unheard of too. It's unthinkable. The need to know what my daughter is doing, and where she is, is making my skin itch.

Chapter ten

The three students are in front of us, laughing and swaying, and it's then that I spy their drinks – two gin and tonics and a vodka and coke in sleek cans; classy chicks, gone are the days of a bottle of White Lightning. Still, they're half pissed already, so the cans have done their job. Christ, it's not even noon.

I want to scold myself for being such a granny about it – I used to do it myself, and yes, I had carefree, fun days. Things are different now. I can't shrug it off and be the 'cool aunt' who cracks a can with them; though I notice Adele is desperate to.

She's walking a notch slower than them and a step faster than me. She wants to be in both worlds: adulthood – and all its sensibility and restrictions – and kidulthood, with all its freedom and public drinking. I get the appeal. I've yearned for it and acted on those impulses myself. While studying in Scotland, I drank and partied with the best of them, but also made sure I wasn't seen as a child… acted like an adult.

Ha! Some adult, Abi, you–

'The girls said the student union was right around the corner.' Adele's excited voice distracts me from my thoughts again. It's getting slightly annoying now. Or maybe her tone is. She's giddy. It's not infectious and welcoming, like it is at work, and I'm mad at her. I'm not entirely sure why I'm mad at her. And actually, it's not just at her. I've stopped in the middle of the pavement, frowning hard, and I feel violent. I never feel this aggressive, but there's a fireball of rage building in my stomach and I want to lash out. What the fuck is wrong with me?

'Abi, are you okay?'

I flinch at her touch, gentle as it is on my forearm. It does go some way towards extinguishing the flames burning inside of me. I take a deep breath and try with every ounce of strength in my body not to sound like a total bitch when I reply.

'Adele, I just need to find my Rose.'

She smiles, oblivious. 'I know, girl, that's why we're here. Let's go in and check it out.'

I follow her, on autopilot, and watch her breeze through the door of the student union. It's as if she's wearing her green uniform – chest pumped high – and she's here to save the day. There's no feeling like that in me. Rather, there's a small and insignificant feeling, like I shouldn't be here, as though I already know Rose isn't here. I continue to follow her anyway.

'Excuse me, coming through,' Adele calls out. Most of the students ignore her.

The bar is rammed. I'd say on an ordinary day this place is quite big, spacious even, but right now it's the exact image you conjure when someone says a gig was packed with people wall to wall, like sardines. I'm a fucking sardine in a student bar. The rage ignites again.

'Let us through, please; give us some room.' Adele continues to try to sound important. She's not, and these people know it. She is creating some kind of pathway and I follow her to the bar where she's shouting my daughter's name at the bartender like we're bloody Cagney and Lacey. 'I'm looking for a Rose Quinn, have you seen her?'

The young lad, obviously a first-year student himself, shrugs – his brown skin is a mirror of Adele's, his youthfulness is not – and points to the array of drinks. That's all he can help her with.

'This is pointless,' I whisper in her ear. 'He can't pick out one student from the hundreds he must see on a daily basis.'

'It's worth a try. Do you want me to order us a drink while I'm here?'

For crying out loud. Seriously?

'Do what you want, Adele. I can't stand here waiting for a pub quiz to start. I'm going to look around for Rose.'

She gives me a thumbs up. 'Good idea. You scope out the place and I'll stay put. If she's here already, she'll need a drink at some point, and if she arrives late, I'll see her. I've got a great line to the door.'

I return the thumbs up with a wildly enthusiastic smile. The sarcasm is lost on my friend. Well, my colleague. This is the reason I don't have friends. I don't have time for them. That sounds awful, doesn't it? I don't have time for any friends… wow. All the woman wants to do is help me. But it's a burden, isn't it? It's not a help. Everything is slower when you have friends, and you have to take into account what they think and what they want to do. Because trust me, if it weren't for Adele, I wouldn't be stuck in this sweaty, bitter-smelling, cramped pub. I'd be inside Rose's house with a warm cup of tea, laughing with my daughter.

So, that's exactly what I'm going to do.

Trying to break through the throngs of people is actually quite difficult now as more undergraduates have arrived en masse for the quiz, and Adele isn't channelling Moses and parting the Red Sea – or perhaps it was God who accomplished that, I forget the details. I let the rage lead me. Head down and arms out, I push my way through to the door and out onto the street. The rain greets me. I let the wet drops pelt my face. It's refreshing, and I can't help standing still for a few moments to let them wash over me. I have no umbrella, but who cares? This is needed. It's dampening my fire.

A black shadow of doubt crosses my mind; what if Rose is in the student union? I'm so busy telling myself I don't need friends and Adele is just getting in the way and blah blah blah, when actually the woman could be right. My daughter could be sat in there, at a table in the far corner, enjoying a pitcher of snakebite and preparing to show off her general knowledge prowess. Why am I so quick to dismiss the idea?

Because a mother flaming well knows, that's why.

My inner voice yells at me and I snap my eyes open. I'm right, of course I am. A parent just knows these things. A mother's instinct – that you receive when the umbilical cord is cut – is the gift from your child when the nurse takes them away to clear the blood and muck that they've clung to as they left your body. It's their way of saying, 'Here, Mum, this will help you when I'm away from home, at whatever age, lost and vulnerable, and need your help. Mother's instinct will lead you to me.'

Somebody help me. What the hell is happening in my head?

I rub my hands up and down over my face, hard and fast, unsure if I'm wiping away the dampness from the rain or trying to rattle some sense into myself. Either way, I need to get moving. Standing here in a downpour talking to myself about a baby's journey through the birth canal is exactly the reason strangers call the paramedics.

The ironic laugh escapes my lips before I have a chance to stop it, adding to the crazed-woman look, of course, and I wish I had my uniform on. Its green starchiness known to everyone – a beacon of hope, if you will – would bring me the strength to face any situation, especially in this moment of weakness.

It's when I look up and take a deep lungful of drizzly air that I see him.

I almost choke, wondering if the rain has blurred my vision as well as my brain. It's him, as clear as day, as my mum used to say – despite this day being anything but clear.

There, casually walking on the other side of the street, wearing a long black funnel coat, dark denim jeans and tanned brogues, and holding a large fisherman-type umbrella – far too big for just one person – is the man I hoped I would never see again.

Chapter eleven

Despite me never wanting to come face to face with him again, my legs start moving of their own accord. I'm slinking along my side of the street, eyes never shifting from his every move, and I have no control over my body. It's as if my hearing has been cut off, locked in a soundproof bizarre bubble that's transported me back in time to when I had done this before: followed him, under the cover of the darkest nights. A sound pierces my protective seal – the heavy rain pounding against the pavement. It splashes up the backs of my legs as they quicken their pace.

I'm back there, in Scotland in my early twenties, watching the man I obsessed over for far longer than I care to admit. He hasn't seen me since that awful night, and a scratching sensation begins to claw inside my chest, working its way to my throat. I remember his temper: the burning fury in his eyes when he caught me in his home. I remember his violence: the way he grabbed a handful of my hair and flung me out the front door. I remember his words: the promise he made to kill me if he ever saw me again.

I stop walking and struggle for air. It no longer feels like lunchtime at the seaside, disturbed only by a little drizzle, but rather that the downpour of rain has brought with it an early night-time. The entire city has somehow been cloaked in a nocturnal shadow, a black beast covering any hopes of sun, eclipsing us completely.

I lean forward slightly, resting my palms on each knee and slowly drinking in the air; deep breaths in through my nose and steadily out through my mouth. The dizzy light-headedness makes me feel sick, and the fear clawing inside me soon turns to a heaving sensation.

'You alright, dear?' a woman's voice says close to my ear. 'Should I call 999 for you?'

I tilt my head skywards, squint against the raindrops, and find an elderly woman wearing an old-fashioned plastic rain cap over her head, gawping at me. She repeats her question, a little murmur like a mouse, and I dismiss her with a shake of my head. The woman means well, I'm sure, but I just want to be on my own.

'Don't have one of those mobile thingies, of course. There's a phone box on the corner, just down there,' she continues, and I realise my head shake meant nothing to her.

I stand up; not in a straight or assertive manner, but it's all the energy I can muster. 'No, it's fine, thank you. I'm fine. I'll be fine. Just need to catch my breath is all.'

The old woman shrugs, as if she doesn't believe me, as if she wants some drama to witness during her walk to the shops in the rain. If only she knew...

I walk away, because I can tell she didn't have any plans to leave me alone, and soon realise that I've made it to the crossing. Looking over the road, I can still see him. Actually, I see him full on – his chiselled jaw and perfect nose, his big pink lips. He's aged in that way that beautiful men do age: they just seem more beautiful. It hits me then. I can see him full on because he's standing on the other side of the street, waiting for the traffic lights to turn red so he can cross the road. So he can walk straight towards me.

Has he noticed it's me?

No, of course he hasn't. He wouldn't recognise me now. It's been over twenty years since he last saw me. I've changed.

But have I really changed?

The beeping sound that signals it's safe to cross begins and the people on the other side of the road start their advance towards me. I take a step back. I focus only on him, and his eyes are trained on me. I think. I mean the umbrella is fucking huge, it's covering the two people either side of him. I'm one hundred per cent – okay ninety per cent – sure his gaze is locked on me.

I take another step back, away from the lip of the kerb, and wait. I don't know what I'm waiting for, but I hear the tuts of strangers as I stand in their way. He walks straight up to me, stands in front of me and smiles. The stupid umbrella is covering me too now – the pair of us are encased in this protection from everything else – and he opens his mouth and says hello. My legs can't take it any more. I half stumble, half collapse, and his free arm instinctively reaches out and holds me up. I feel his warmth, his strength, and the fear inside me evaporates. I'm twenty again, in the arms of the man I love.

'I thought that was you,' he whispers in my ear, and his words are smooth; smooth as silk caressing my skin. 'I can't believe you're standing in front of me, Abi. What are you doing here?'

How does he do that? How does his voice have so much power and control and authority that I'm literally stood here – a full-grown woman of forty – feeling like a teenager paralysed by love? My hands are trembling, my lips are quavering, and I can't string a fucking sentence together.

'So, you're obviously as surprised to see me as I am to see you,' he says with a thick Glaswegian accent, and gently lifts me off his arm slightly.

The movement corrects my posture, forcing me to regain some control over my own body, and I look directly in his eyes. I see Rose. Her face fills my mind, and it gives me the strength to pull myself together. I take a deep breath, wipe the moisture from my face and clear my throat.

'Patrick… surprised is an understatement,' I finally reply, but it doesn't sound like me. It's as if I've been on a long flight and my ears haven't popped. I have to continue now – I can't let him know he's leaving me tongue-tied and dry-mouthed. 'I thought you said you would never leave Glasgow, that it was your home and where your family are.'

I stop myself at the image of his family, the pain of that night returning. He notices it too. I see it in his face. Something has changed about him. He doesn't seem pained by the memory.

'That was a long time ago,' he says, 'and after… well, after that night, it was difficult to stay in Scotland. Sadie wanted to be closer to her family, you know, for support, and–'

'You're here with Sadie?' The tempo of my voice has risen. 'What do you mean, after that night? Are you saying you've been in Brighton for twenty years?'

His long eyelashes flutter and his mouth opens and closes a few times before he manages, 'Well, no, not twenty years. Almost, though. It's just–'

'I didn't know your wife's family lived in Brighton.' I can't tell if the trickle down my neck is sweat or rain; realistically, I know it can't be rain because of this damn umbrella canopying us – which is actually starting to suffocate me. My hands tremble again, but this time it isn't out of fear. 'You've been down here all this time, Patrick? I… I…'

He sighs and uses the thumb and forefinger on his free hand to furiously rub his eyelids. Why am I still standing here? Why am I watching him?

Duck out from under this bloody brolly and walk away. Just walk away, Abi.

The heartache and lies and fear that come with this man are too painful to even contemplate reliving.

He shrugs his large shoulders and I can't help but think I see a small smile dancing on his lips. 'Have a drink with me, Abi.'

It's more of a statement than a question. It's how Patrick always spoke to me. Except I never used to mind when I was nineteen, twenty, twenty-one. I did as he said. Now, words won't surface to my lips, so a single shake of my head is all I give him.

'Abi, please.' Oh God, the way he says my name. 'Let me explain. We have so much to talk about. And I know this quaint little pub not far from here. No students ever go near it; you'll just love it, I know you will. It'll be quiet. It'll be nice. We can talk about everything. Please.'

I gulp; the simple act of swallowing saliva feels like the biggest task I've ever taken on. Where's the Abigail Quinn who dashes into the unknown on a daily basis? Where's the paramedic who rescues strangers without so much as a trembling finger? Where's the woman who restarted her life single-handedly?

'This is fate, us meeting like this after all this time, Abi. Please.'

Oh, Patrick, you have to stop begging me. I'm not strong enough to say no to you. I never was. Plus, I don't know if I want to talk about everything.

Yes, I want to know why he and his flaming wife are living in Brighton, but if he tells me, if I hear too much from him, will I confess my secrets too? Secrets that I just can't afford to confess? As I look at the most handsome face I've ever known, I suddenly don't trust myself at all.

Chapter twelve

We're in the pub, of course we are, because we all knew I would say yes to Patrick. I can't remember a time when I wouldn't say yes to this man, and here we are, over twenty years since the last time we laid eyes on each other, and we've fallen back into our roles perfectly. I hate myself for it. But I love how it's making me feel, like I'm eighteen again; with the carefree attitude of a new student who's just moved to Glasgow Caledonian University, ready to embrace a degree in Paramedic Science and save the new city I had come to love.

It was in the early days of my studies when I first met Patrick. I don't think he noticed me straight away, if I'm honest. He caught me like a punch to the abdomen that knocks the air right out of you. Like the time I fell from that tree and couldn't breathe but I knew I was alive; that's how he made me feel just before my nineteenth birthday. Part of my degree was practice-based education within the Scottish Ambulance Service – or SAS for short – and there he was playing the hero I had always wanted to be. He was only part-time, however, due to a long-standing injury to his back. He used to blame the job – but never in a way that made him sound like he hated it. He seemed to love helping people. He loved people. Patrick was making the transition from paramedic to mentor, and it began with my academic year.

He was older. Fifteen years my senior, and that full head of salt-and-pepper hair gave him an authority, and a sexiness, that I couldn't ignore. Those sapphire eyes could drink in every part of you, like they really saw you when you spoke, and invited you to step into his ocean – into his bubble – and see only him in return. Full lips that spoke with such enthusiasm and passion they could cause a knot in your stomach. A knot of desire, of fear, of excitement. Who knows which feeling? Perhaps all of them, and that explains the hold he had over me. When I was with him, he could make me feel every single emotion – and utter numbness just as fast.

What I do know for sure is, all those years ago, he had me at 'Welcome to the SAS'. I knew in that very moment I had to have him. The thrill of learning my craft through my degree and snaring the man who'd caught my heart was everything I yearned for. It didn't matter what I had to do to succeed in both goals. And I did succeed, for a short while, but at a cost.

'So, what do you think? This is a great little pub, isn't it? Quaint,' Patrick says, breaking through my memories and placing our drinks on the table: a pint of Guinness for him and a large red for me.

I can't stop the internal glow that comes with his simple action, an action we must have shared a hundred times before. The two of us, in a *quaint* pub – as he keeps referring to it anyway, when we both know what that really translates to is small and dark and where no one will notice or question us – huddled over our drinks, whispering. I never cared much for Guinness, though Patrick often tried to make me like it. During my pregnancy with Rose, I did have one half of the black stuff – good for the iron levels, Mum told me – but I hated it. Probably because I hated the memory it conjured.

He's watching me. Waiting. So, I play the game and gaze around the small public house with its low, beamed ceiling. There's a fire roaring to the right of us, and I'm actually thankful for it as it's drying my soaked body. The lighting is low and dim, as if the light bulbs aren't light bulbs at all, but small candles encased in glass and on the verge of dying. I couldn't describe the man sat just two tables away from me if I tried. That might be the appeal of this place to Patrick, and I briefly wonder how often he comes here. Books stand in rows on the shelves behind him – the old kind, with navy and burgundy hardback covers, spiralling gold letters down the spine, and dusty cream pages.

'Yes, it's a lovely little place,' I finally reply, and he wipes the white froth from his top lip as he smiles. My stomach spins. 'Do you come here often?'

Okay, I officially hate myself for that line.

'Yes,' he says, the smile still in place. 'It's nice to drink where the students don't.'

I sip my own beverage, realising I haven't eaten much, and quickly hope the wine only brings on a headache and not a full lowering of my inhibitions. After another gulp, I return the glass to the table and nod in agreement.

'Yes, I can imagine. I was actually just in the student union with a friend… She's looking for someone. But it got so crowded and stuffy in there, I had to get out.'

'That's when I found you like a drowned rat on the street?'

Oh God. His voice. His accent. It's bringing everything back and something inside me stirs. I smile and take another drink. My fingers shake around the glass. I hope he hasn't noticed.

'So, come on, what are you doing here?' he asks.

The fruity red liquid runs down the wrong hole and I splutter for a moment. I don't want to talk. I want to listen to him. Not even just for his voice, but because I need to know what the hell *he's* doing here.

When I steady my breathing, I bat the question back and say, 'Really, Patrick? We're in Brighton, half an hour from London, where we know I was born and bred. Where you knew I moved back to. If anyone has the right to ask "what are you doing here", it's me.'

I'm surprised by the gumption in my voice. It's bloody good to know the new ballsy Abi – as Adele described me – has actually come along for the journey. It makes me sit a little taller, and I cross one leg over the other and lean back in my chair slightly, watching him.

Patrick mirrors my body language, adding a half-smile to his full lips, as if he's submitting to me. The stir I felt just moments before travels a little south of my stomach now, and a tingling sensation takes over. I feel the new Abi is looking at me with pure disgust.

Yes, I hate myself too.

'Well, as I said, Sadie felt she wanted to be closer to her family. I mean after…'

'After she found out about me.' I finish Patrick's sentence, because he obviously can't possibly bring himself to say it. I can't help rolling my eyes as I do.

'Yes, of course, Abi. You know she took the news about us really badly.'

'The news,' I echo, slightly louder than needed. 'I don't think walking in on us in her martial bed is classed as a newsworthy revelation. More of a life-changing moment, and an unfortunate time for her to have to come home early – sick from work if I recall?'

If I recall… Who the hell am I trying to sound like? I remember that day as clear as anything.

'Yes, well, that day–'

'How is Ms Banks?' I cut him off, not because I want to be rude, but because the pain in my chest is crushing me, and I'm not sure if I can control the tears or push them down any further if Patrick insists on going over that day in more detail.

'Sadie is fine, thank you for asking. She doesn't go by her maiden name any longer,' he says with a slight grin, but I see the twitch in his jaw.

He used to hate the fact that his wife refused to use her marital surname, back when I knew them anyway. Sadie had made a name for herself as a successful romance author before they were married and believed changing her surname would undo all her hard work. I would pander to Patrick's ego back then, telling him I would do anything to have his name and would shout from the rooftops if we were married. He thought I was joking, but the sex after that conversation would always be amazing. The truth is, I meant it.

'She hasn't published anything of late, I've noticed.' No point in pretending I hadn't always looked for her books in the supermarkets or on Amazon.

Patrick takes a large gulp from his pint and shakes his head. 'She never wrote a single word again after that night.'

My lips twist into a scolding pout. 'No, I guess it's hard to write about the joys of love when you find your husband's been shagging a local student.'

I'm shocked by my tone. If Patrick is, he doesn't say anything. A slow huff is all he releases before saying, 'No, she was busy with other things.'

I frown and idly fumble with the stem of my wine glass. It's not so much what he said, but the way in which he said it that prompts my next question – though it feels a struggle to get any words out at all, thanks to the tightness in my chest. 'Wh-what do you… what do you mean?'

'Sadie was pregnant when she found the two of us together, and we moved here to start our family,' Patrick blurts out.

And there they are, the words I expected… yet the very ones I didn't want to hear. The heaviness inside me becomes a mound of glue trying to move through my body, suffocating my throat and crushing my heart.

'I wanted to tell you, Abi. Really, I did. But what would have been the point? You made it clear you were leaving for London.'

'Because you made it clear you were staying with her.' I choke out the words, hardly recognising my own voice.

'Abi, she tried to commit suicide that night, you know that. We forced Sadie to do such a thing. She was willing to take her own life, and my child's life, because of what we did to her. What we made her witness. What we–'

I hold up my hand to make him stop talking. I can't look him in the face. Hot tears run down my cheeks. Not gushing like waves; they're slow and burn like bubbling lava.

After I ran from their home that night, alone and scared, I begged Patrick to meet me the next morning. He had told me about Sadie, about what she had done to herself with the razor blades, and I felt guilt like never before. He said then, as he's just said now, that it was what *we* had done. Even twenty odd years ago, I didn't truly believe that. It was what *I* had done. *I* had seen Patrick and *I* had wanted him. *I* had followed and seduced and tempted a married man. *I* broke that woman. When it became all too clear that Patrick didn't really want me, and that a woman's life had been ruined because of it in the process, I made the decision to leave Scotland for good. He never admitted then that Sadie was pregnant, just as I failed to admit that I was too.

'But… you always said that you didn't want children. You didn't want a family. You were too old to start a family. That's what you said to me.' The words roll off my tongue like a steam train, my voice sounding like that of a child's.

Patrick reaches over the table and lightly touches my hand, obviously unsure if I'll pull it away. I don't. 'I didn't want a family, Abi. For Christ's sake, I was thirty-six years old at that point. It was something I never wanted to start then.'

'I remember.'

'But what was I to do? I had to do the right thing. The right thing by Sadie. We'd already caused her so much pain. So much so that she was ready to kill our unborn child. I had to be there for her. And the baby. I had to be the husband and father she and my child needed.'

'The right thing by Sadie?' His words rattle inside my brain. 'What about the right thing by me?'

He sighs and squeezes his fingers tighter around mine. 'Oh, Abi, I cared for you, I did. And I think if Sadie never found out about us, we would have carried on for a long, long time. But it wouldn't have been right–'

'What about your baby?' I interrupt, the volcano fully ready to erupt.

A proud smile oozes onto his face and I hate myself for feeling the way I do towards an innocent child. 'Sadie accepted my apology, and my promise that it would never happen again, but she couldn't stay in Scotland around my friends and family. Around the memories of what you and I had done in our home. Her condition was that we moved here to Brighton, where her mum and dad and brother live.'

Patrick had never told me that. I'd never known that my rival's family lived just half an hour's train journey away from me and mine. All that time.

'Later that year,' he continued, 'just after we moved into our new home by the seafront, Sadie gave birth to—'

'I didn't mean that baby,' I say through gritted teeth, fuming at the idyllic family life painting he's parading in front of me.

His grip loosens slightly, though he doesn't move his hand, and he frowns. That look in his brooding eyes… Now he feels it. It's not so much what I've said, but the way in which I've said it. 'W-what… what do you mean, Abi?'

'I mean, later that same year, after I had to move back in with my parents, when I gave birth to a baby. Your baby.'

Patrick yanks his hand from mine, the overspill of the hot lava burning his skin as well as mine, and the red flush from the warm fire drains from his cheeks. His mouth opens and closes, and he says nothing. What can he say?

I understand the numb feeling that's taking over his body because it's taking over mine too. The lines etched on his forehead, the pool of tears in his eyes, the dryness of his mouth and the tremble of his whole body – it's a mirror reflection of my own. Patrick must be crushed to discover he has another child. I'm crushed to discover Rose has been in the same vicinity as her father for almost a year.

The father I told her had died in the line of duty months before she was born.

Chapter thirteen

I don't know why it was that particular story I chose to use as a lie. It wasn't something planned out to the very last detail, and I didn't exactly know where it would go; it really did snowball out of control.

Rose was coming up to her fourth birthday when I decided, when I knew what needed to be done. She was in a part-time private nursery, between our home and my parents' house, and I was in my element – finally a fully fledged paramedic. After leaving Scotland, deciding that I was in fact keeping the baby growing inside of me, and giving birth to Rose later that year, I then had to complete a three-week induction into the London Ambulance Service with a clinical tutor.

It felt so good to not have wasted my degree. My parents were supportive of all my decisions and doted on Rose, of course. Only Mum knew the truth about Patrick – about the married man I'd had an affair with – and Dad didn't ask many questions. They rarely do, do they, dads? They're happy with minimal information, rarely prodding and poking for the finer details, unlike some mothers who need chapter and verse, from what you ate to what time you got home. Which is exactly what my mother needed. The woman who could spot a half story from a mile away and demanded to know the full truth before she could even begin to play along. That's where me and my mum are identical in our parenting ways. Maybe it comes with only having one child – the *need* to know absolutely everything about them.

My mind briefly conjures the memory of the voicemail Rose left me during the terrorist attack, and the name Dylan circles round and round in my head. I think of all the friends' numbers that I have… not a single one. I'm overcome with a feeling of hate towards myself, no one else. Here I am, thinking I'm so like my mother, with our shared desire to know everything about our daughters and yet, when I'm being tested, I find myself not knowing the exact things I need to bloody know.

I try to shake off the frustration that's building strength in my neck and travelling north to my temples. I picture my father again; a man who was just happy to have his only daughter home once more. Rose was a delightful bonus to him. He was so proud of me, working hard and putting into practice in London what I'd learnt in Scotland – I was proud too. It felt good. London was my home, and I couldn't remember why I had craved so intensely to leave it, or why Scotland had appealed to me so much. But then, isn't that always the way when a chapter in our lives ends tragically? It's impossible to look back on it with any comfort or fondness.

Anyway, niggles of questions had started with Rose: she wanted to know what a daddy was, and why her friend Natalie lived with a man and a woman, yet she only lived with me. I had danced around it for long enough; those questions were only going to intensify, and they did. Father's Day arrived and Rose's nursery used this occasion to make cards and finger paintings and superhero drawings, and all of that other crap that makes children focus on their daddies.

Oh God, I know I shouldn't think that way. It wasn't the damn nursery's fault.

Nonetheless, Rose didn't really know what it all meant, so she made a lovely card for her granddaddy – wise beyond her years, that girl, I'll tell you, but sadly some kids aren't, and those monsters are the ones who become high school bullies. Rose came home and cried. The kids had told her she had to make a card for her daddy, not her granddad because that wasn't the same. Her little face was red and blotchy, and the snot trickled down to her small lips uncontrollably. To a four-year-old, being different can be hard.

'Why, Mum? Why? Why don't I have a dad? All the kiddies at school have dads and I don't. Why, Mum? Why?' Rose's small voice choked as she questioned me over and over again. She breathed in deeply, her pebble-brown eyes masked by tears, and she looked up at me, waiting. Waiting for an answer. Waiting for an explanation. Waiting for a reason.

As the parent, it's your job to have all the answers.

It was in that moment I knew I couldn't do this for the rest of our lives. Yes, the older she got, the more Rose would understand. The older she got, the more kids and teenagers and friends there would be who had no dad, or no mum, or two dads, or two mums, or step-parents, or extended families – especially living in such a diverse city as London. But all I could see, right there in that instance, was my daughter's crumpled face desperate to understand why she was… *different*. And so, I did what any parent would do. I scooped her up in my arms and I made everything better for her.

I told Rose about a man – a hero – who died before she was born. I told her about a firefighter who I met in Scotland and loved dearly, who saved people's lives on a daily basis and taught many students how to do the same. I told my daughter she didn't have a daddy because he had died rescuing someone else.

It didn't sound too dishonest when I first uttered those words, the words that calmed and soothed her and allowed her to understand why everyone's families are not the same. Patrick was a paramedic who I met in Scotland and loved dearly. Patrick saved lives and taught many students how to do the same. Patrick died to me when he chose to save his marriage and stay with his wife. It wasn't the worst lie in the world.

That's what got me through it.

As Rose got older she would occasionally ask a few questions, mainly on holidays like the dreaded Father's Day, or sometimes even on her own birthday. From an early stage I made it quite clear it was something that hurt me to talk about. She could obviously see the pain in my eyes because she never pushed me too far.

Over the years I added on a bit more information to keep her at bay from ever digging too deep: I didn't know her father's family because he was quite a bit older than me; he was cremated so there was no grave to visit; returning to Scotland would be too painful for me and was something I never wanted to do.

I don't know why – and I never wanted to ask – but from about the age of fifteen, Rose seemed to accept everything I had said. She stopped asking about her father, but every Father's Day, she would give me a bunch of flowers to say thank you for playing both roles in her life, and she would ask if there was anything I wanted to do or talk about. The answer was always no. I didn't want to rock the boat. Her annual gesture made my heart both swell with love and pride and break with guilt and shame.

I raised an amazing daughter – an amazing woman – but it all started with a lie. A lie that has gone on for so long, the truth can never be told because I know that if I do, I will lose my daughter forever.

Chapter fourteen

Patrick's looking at me with those same sad eyes, demanding answers and explanations, and I'm positive that I can see a glimmer of moisture in them. Patrick isn't a crier – at least he wasn't when I knew him – and I can't help feeling that shame all over again.

I want to get up and run; this small, shabby place has become a claustrophobic dome, the fire having sucked the life out of it, and all I can feel is the heat on my skin. It's burning my neck and my eyeballs and singeing every hair on my head.

'Abi!'

His voice drags me from the pit of flames, supports me like a water buoy, and I rapidly suck in a lungful of air in fear of the fire snatching it away from me again. But it doesn't. I'm okay, I can breathe, and my body hasn't combusted in a rage of fire.

'How… how did I not know about this?' Patrick says, the quiver of his lips and chin unmissable.

I half-laugh, half-sigh at his look of misery. 'Like I knew about all the things you've just told me, Patrick. Are you being serious?'

He slowly exhales and rubs both hands over his face. Perhaps he's hoping for some magic trick, that I'll have disappeared by the time he's finished. It's debatable. I don't need his pain on my conscience too.

Wait a minute. He's the bloody reason I lied to Rose in the first place.

I feel the irritation prickling at me. 'You know, Patrick, if you were honest with me twenty years ago… if you had told me about Sadie and the little family that you had decided on starting, and the fact you left Scotland to live in Brighton–'

'Hang on,' he interrupts. 'Why are you in Brighton?'

Now it's my turn to pray for a magic trick. But what's the use? It won't help me. 'Rose… our daughter… attends Brighton University. She's almost finished her first year.'

Patrick steeples his hands in front of his face, as if he's praying. I know no amount of praying or magic can help us now. Any colour left in his face drains away. He's grey. As grey as that thunderous sky outside. He runs his hands over his forehead, then his fingers glide through his neat hair – I notice a soft tug to the strands as he does so – and he stares down at the table.

'I know what you're thinking,' I say, trying to break the suffocating silence between us, although I have no fucking clue what he's thinking. I don't even know what I'm thinking. 'You could have bumped into her or you could have passed each other on the street, on the beach, anywhere. You have to understand – how could I have ever known you were here?'

In that moment, it occurs to me that I have no idea what Patrick does for work here. I would say his time on the ambulances is far behind him…

'Oh my God, Patrick, do you work at the university?'

He lifts his head, but it remains firmly in his hands, as if he doesn't have the strength to hold it up; but he does manage to bob it up and down. Slowly. He huffs. 'Yes, Abi, I work there. In the science department. The university has different campuses spread across Brighton. What does she… our… Rose, did you say? That's a nice name. What does Rose study?'

'English Literature.' The words come out as a whisper.

Patrick breathes differently this time. It's not a huff or a puff, but a release of some kind. I can tell the difference just as I see a smile tug on his lips. 'That's studied on a different campus to mine,' he says. 'Okay, it's not a million miles away, but as a part-time Paramedic Science tutor, I've never had the need to venture there. Hopefully your daughter has had no need to come across to mine.'

Goosebumps bristle my skin at the way he says 'your daughter', but what do I expect? He's just found out about Rose; there's hardly going to be any admiration in his tone.

'Yes, hopefully not,' I concur, and have no more words.

The dryness of my mouth reaches my throat and I feel like I've taken part in one of those dry cracker eating competitions. Where do we go from here? What do I do? I can't tell Rose the truth after all these years.

'Actually, I haven't been able to get in touch with Rose.' I drain my wine glass, allowing the scarlet liquid to warm my throat and bring some normality to my mouth. 'It's the reason I'm here at all. She hasn't answered her phone to me for a couple of days.' I try to downplay it, outwardly seem cool and at ease, when in truth, I feel like I'm drowning without even the hope of a paddle to save me.

'You travelled to your daughter's uni because she hadn't answered the phone?' Patrick says and laughs. 'Imagine your mother doing that when you were in Scotland. Jesus, Abi, you would have gone ballistic.'

I hate him; no, I hate his words. But is that because he has a point?

'She's a grown woman. A student. What are you expecting, daily updates on her activities?' he continues, a patronising smirk on his lips and deep furrows in his brow.

He thinks I'm overreacting, just as Dave and Adele did. What's wrong with these people? Or is it that there's something wrong with me?

'Well…' I hesitate. 'It's just, I mean, Rose and I are very close, and we speak regularly. To not hear from her is strange. For crying out loud, why is that so difficult for everyone to understand?' The frustration is tiptoeing on anger.

Patrick raises a hand and removes the smirk. At least that's something. 'I'm sorry,' he says, 'I didn't mean to upset you. Of course, it's natural to worry when your kid leaves home and gets a life for themselves, especially when you were the biggest part of their lives. Take it from someone who knows. Not only am I a parent who lost their kid to university, but I see it every year when freshers hit the halls. They grow up, Abi. They do their own thing.'

He's right. They're all right. But I can't shake the worry that has taken root in the pit of my stomach, pushing aside logic and reason. It's bad enough trying to ignore Patrick's continual use of 'my kid' and 'your kid' – another kick to my already vulnerable gut.

'She hasn't even been on social media for two days. And there was a terrorist attack in London on Friday, in case you don't get the news down here by the sunshiny seaside…' Now I sound like the child – not even because it's far from sunny here today – so I pause to take a deep breath. 'She would have been worried about me and wanted to check in.'

God, I sound desperate. I must look it too because Patrick takes my hand in his again. The warmth of his skin brings those goosebumps back for all the wrong reasons.

'Abi, listen to me.' Oh God, the way my name rolls off his Scottish tongue. 'I know you're worried, and I didn't mean to make you feel like your thoughts or feelings don't matter. Rose is just doing what any twenty-year-old does during their first year at university. She's enjoying herself, probably doing things she's never done before and meeting people that are blowing her mind. Just like you did in Scotland. Don't deny her that by storming down here and making her feel guilty for not checking in on you.'

I actually never thought of it like that. Looking back, she had tried to check on me that afternoon during the attack. It was me who didn't get back to her. I nod, concluding he's right. I pull my hand away from his; the power he holds over me is infuriating.

He gets it. He gets me. I can see it in the way he pulls his shoulders taller and clears his throat.

'Okay, now we need some damage limitation.' Patrick's voice pierces through my personal doubts. His heavy head is no more and the colour in his cheeks has returned. 'Your daughter… Rose… can't find out about me. And my family can't find out about her. Maybe if this happened when we had just moved here, if we had all known the truth then there could have been a way to deal with it… to all be in each other's lives. But it's been twenty years, Abi, and too many people would get hurt. We have to stay away from one another.'

I nod along, unable to formulate any words. Mental tiredness; it must be that. I shudder at the image of Patrick playing happy families with *them*… his family who are not me and Rose. He's saying there's a chance that things could have been different. If only that were true.

'Do you agree that's the best for everyone?'

I continue to nod along like a toy puppy stationed at the back of someone's car. Patrick is right – deep down I know he is – but it still stings. He's still a family man: his wife and child come first, just like they did twenty years ago. It's then I realise that I have to do the same. I, too, need to put my own family first.

I have to continue with this lie. There's no choice – regardless of the fact that Patrick is sat here in front of me. I have to continue with this lie because I'm not about to ruin my daughter's life.

Chapter fifteen

The light attacks my eyes as soon as I step out of the public house, and it takes a minute to focus. The rain has eased to a drizzle on its farewell journey, and the street is still cloaked in a wintery darkness, but the fresh, cold air and general buzz of life which has continued to take place outside is a shock to the system.

Patrick decided not to leave with me. There was no more for me to say. I think we had both said enough, both agreed on a way forward for now. There were no grand goodbyes or swapping of numbers, no promises to keep in touch or see each other again soon. It seemed the right thing to do as I stood from the table and explained I had to leave. Now it feels strange. I feel empty after having made no plans. What plans could we make? Except the most important one of keeping this charade in place. He said he would have another pint before making his way home. I translated that to mean at least ten more pints; that's definitely what I would do if I just found out I had a secret love child living in the same town as me.

A chilly breeze whips around my face and ears and neck, blowing cold whispers on my skin – it's welcoming after the stuffiness of the confined space now behind me. As welcoming as it is, I can't ignore that there's a decision to be made. Do I continue my search for Rose, or do I return home?

Before I can decide, my mobile pings with what sounds like a hundred notifications. It seems the dinginess of the pub not only clouded my senses, but also my reception. I pull the phone from my pocket and gasp when I see all the messages and missed calls from Adele; I had completely forgotten about her.

My friend is worried, of course she is, and not only about me but Rose too; one message even asks if we're at the local hospital. My tendency to overreact is becoming infectious. I check the time and realise I've been gone for over an hour; amazing how times flies when you're stuck in the past and confessing your sins. I thumb over the screen in order to form a reply to Adele. My mind's still not clear on which direction to take. Then I hear Patrick's words and I can't shake them away: *'Don't deny her that by storming down here and making her feel guilty for not checking in on you.'*

Is that really what I'm doing here? Am I so mad at Rose for not checking in with me, not seeing how I am after the ordeal at work, that I've somehow turned it all on its head and made it seem like she's the one in the wrong? In the wrong or missing… I don't feel so sure now. If Patrick thinks that about me – and Adele and Dave, too; they just weren't as blunt as my ex-lover – then maybe they're right.

Rather than dance around the decision any longer, I call Adele – the relief in her voice is deafening – and tell her I'll meet her at the train station. We'll get the first train back to London, and I may even treat her to dinner somewhere closer to home to say sorry, or thank you… well, both really. I don't know if she's pleased about the thought of a free meal or the fact that I've got in touch with her so she can regale me with tales of her student pub quiz experience, but either way, I'm glad she's here. She'll take my mind off Patrick on the journey home. Not that she'll know about that, of course.

I bury my head, tucking my chin into the fleece tunnel of my coat, and brace myself against the wind. Yes, I've said let's go home, and yes, I've told both Patrick and Adele that I'll leave Rose be until she gets in touch with me… but there's still a heaviness in my stomach that I can't shift, no matter how much I try to convince myself otherwise.

A mother just knows, right?

The second decision is made quicker: once I'm alone tonight, I'll search through Rose's Facebook page and find her housemate

Penny on her friends list – possibly even this Dylan guy too. If my daughter has lost her phone, perhaps one of her friends have posted something. Failing that, I'll just send Penny a little line on Messenger asking her to tell Rose to contact her worrying mother. I'll make it light-hearted and innocent sounding. It'll give me some peace… for now, at least.

* * *

The vibration of the van's engine rumbles beneath me. I switch on the blue lights, and Adele races the ambulance along the high street. As always, our siren's shrieks have the desired effect and the vehicles in front do their best to part like a theatre's opening curtains, giving us a clear run of the road. This time, we're halted at traffic lights.

'Come on, come on,' Adele mumbles while trying to mount the kerb.

We both swapped our shifts, so we're working a Monday afternoon to cover Dave and Laura. It doesn't matter to me; I barely know my Mondays from my Saturdays. This job is my routine and sometimes I think I would happily work a shift every day. I did find it strange Adele agreed to come in a day earlier than her rota requested. I have a feeling she's keeping an eye on me. I don't know why; she needn't bother. I'm fine.

'Finally,' she calls out as the lights switch to green and the traffic opens up for us again. 'ETA is eight minutes.'

We've been requested by the police to attend a domestic abuse scene; from the details received so far, the wife sounds to be in a bit of a state and the husband legged it when he spotted the uniform. Adele powers on along Mansfield Road, towards Gospel Oak, and I take a moment to glance at my mobile.

For the past twelve hours it's been within grabbing reach the entire time, and even though the phone hasn't made a pinging sound, I keep checking it. No notifications are coming through. It's on loud, I've turned the volume up to the highest setting, but my eyes continually dart to it and my finger flicks it from 'silent' back to 'ringer on' a few times each hour. You know, just to be sure my phone isn't playing tricks on me. I found Penny through Rose's Facebook contacts and I sent her a message: bright and breezy, like I promised myself. I thought young people were on their phones 24/7, ready to shoot off a reply or emoji or GIF. Not the ones I'm trying to bloody contact. Nothing from my daughter and nothing from Penny regarding Rose. I've picked all the skin from around my unmanicured nails.

'Well, I needn't ask which house number,' Adele comments, and I slip my phone into my side trouser pocket – where I can best feel it vibrate – and look up to the flats she's parking in front of. 'Two squad cars and a van seems a bit much, no?'

'Hmm,' I mumble. 'Could emphasise the damage this man has done. They're waving us in. Let's go find out for ourselves.'

We each grab our response bags and follow a uniformed officer into the main entrance of the flats. The lift is broken, the copper informs us, so we climb the three flights of dark and dingy steps. The stains on the stone ground could be anything, but the stench of warm piss leaves little to the imagination. You see all types of homes in this job; the best thing I've learnt is to say nothing and judge no one. It makes life easier when trying to forge a relationship with the patient.

What doesn't make life easier is walking into a situation and discovering you know the patient.

Entering flat twelve is actually a pleasant surprise, as we find it clean and tidy, and the owner is obviously house-proud. It smells nothing like the rank corridor outside – obviously a citrus fresh Zoflora-loving person lives here – and the three of us walk through a gleaming and uncluttered corridor into a compact, perfectly functional kitchen.

My heart rate quickens to a thumping drum inside my chest; a sound so loud to my ears, I'm convinced everyone else in the room can hear it. It's not beating double time because the woman cowering at the slim breakfast bar is sobbing and shaking, and it's certainly not due to the river of blood gushing from her head – which seems unstoppable against the measly tissues she's holding against the wound – but it's because the woman is Josie Robertson.

For crying out loud, what's happening this week? I feel like Scrooge being visited by the ghosts of Christmas past... It's just my rotten luck to be visited by all the Scottish ones.

Twenty years is a long time. Unfortunately for me, I have one of those faces that doesn't change. If you saw photos of me from nursery through to university you would understand – you can just tell it's me from child to woman.

'Ab-Abi Quinn,' Josie stutters through the tears. 'Is that you? My God, I knew you'd make it.'

For the second time in as many days, the thick Scottish accent does something to my insides; my stomach lurches and a charged shiver runs through my body like an electric current.

Adele and the copper turn to me and frown.

'Josie and I studied Paramedic Science at university together.' I don't want to say too much. Thankfully it's never really been a subject Adele was interested in prying into, and it would be better for all those involved if that doesn't change.

Josie lets out a gurgle of a laugh. It's such a sad noise, as if she's mocking herself. 'Yeah, we did, didn't we, Abi? And look at me now...' She raises her arms in the air, the open cut to her head still oozing blood, the purple bruising to her left eye visible – as is the dry crust of blood in the corner of her mouth. 'I'm the one needing to call the fucking paramedics instead of turning up to help poor souls like... like me.'

As I thought, she is mocking herself. Who can blame her? Adele says nothing and moves closer to Josie, addressing the deep wound on our patient's head and face. Despite the fiery-red hair matted together by the blood, it's clear to see that the cut will need gluing together and a trip to the hospital will be called for.

The other two police officers in the kitchen ask Josie a few more questions about her husband and where he might have gone. She mumbles and grunts her replies, explaining this isn't the first time he's hurt her and that she knows it won't be the last. I feel sorry for the female officer who's trying to reassure Josie that her husband will be arrested for what he's done to her today.

'Whatever,' Josie replies, and her gaze settles on me; they resemble two dark pebbles you'd collect at the beach – stained and wet from the sea but cold and emotionless. 'Bet you never expected to walk in and find me sitting here.'

'Always expect the unexpected in this job, eh?' I reply with a smile, hating myself; I don't want to get into a conversation with Josie.

'I wouldn't know, Abi. I never made it. Not like you obviously did.'

Her comment sounds mean and sarcastic, and from the look of her glass-pebble eyes it'd be easy to think it was. But there's a sadness in her voice that I can't ignore, and my heart goes out to the crumbling woman I see before me. The woman who, in her early twenties, slipped her arm through mine and promised to show me a good time in her city, which she did to the fullest. Josie was the first at any party – and the last to leave, as the saying goes – but she was also the first to hand in her assignments, to check in on her friends and make sure they were doing okay. She radiated warmth. Not like this woman. I don't know this woman.

'Well, I never expected you to move to London, Josie, that's for sure.'

'Followed the scumbag of a man that I now call my husband,' she replies, and tries to smile, but the wince on her face shows it isn't an action she should be doing.

'I'm sorry.' *How pathetic. I'm sorry... really?* That's all I have to say.

Adele finishes cleaning Josie's face and has gauzed the cut as best she can. The police are bustling around us, talking in hushed voices.

'I did think of looking you up, you know,' Josie says, bringing my attention back to her. 'But it was a few years after you left

Scotland, and I didn't really know how to go about it. You never said where you lived exactly.'

I offer a shrug and nod my head. 'London is a big place, Josie. I understand. We all moved on.'

'Yeah, but you just up and left. I always wondered what became of you, Abi. I should have known you would have been in this role. The rising star at uni, the paramedic by nature. What about Patrick?'

Josie's question throws me. The officers are waiting to escort us from the flat to the ambulance and Adele's staring at me too. Why are they all waiting for my answer? *Let's just leave, we all have jobs to do.* What possessed her to ask me that? I was never up front with any of my friends about Patrick. I guess if anyone had cottoned on to the affair, it would have been Josie. Shit, does she know?

'I… err… What do you mean?'

A real smile – albeit small and weak – graces Josie's face for the first time. 'Oh please, Abi, like I didn't know. Don't worry, I think you hid it well; but I could see how much you loved him. Then when I found out he had left Scotland not long after you, I put two and two together and assumed you left because you were–'

'Patrick died,' I blurt out, the consequences of my words catching up moments too late. What if Josie knows he didn't die? What if she knows he's actually only living in Brighton?

Fuck!

'Oh, Abi, I'm so sorry. I had no idea,' she says, and finally stands to leave the kitchen. 'I hadn't heard… haven't really kept in contact with anyone or kept abreast of life after university. Ray never would have allowed me to. He doesn't like me talking to people he doesn't know.' Josie points to her face, as if to explain what she means.

'No, don't apologise,' I continue. 'Well, I mean, the decision to leave Scotland was for me. And my parents. It was the right thing to do because they needed me. I heard on the grapevine about Patrick. Don't know the details or anything. It was a long time ago.' I lose count of the number of lies and obviously feel like I need to add some truth to it because my mouth won't stop moving. 'My dad had cancer and my mother still suffers with dementia now.'

Josie raises her eyebrows. 'Wow, Abi, that's a lot to deal with. I'm glad you still managed to follow your dream and become a paramedic though.'

'Thanks. Me too.' I smile and walk out of the kitchen in a daze.

What is wrong with me? The last job I was at, the woman called me a hero. I'm no one's bloody hero. A bare-faced liar, that's truly what I am.

The sound of voices around me diminishes as I leave the flat; the dank smell of outside isn't even enough to wake my senses. My body is on autopilot, my feet carrying me down the stairs and towards the ambulance through some kind of robotic command. I don't even turn around to see if Adele and Josie are following me, or if the officers are still with us.

I don't care.

I just need to get away from Josie before I feel the need to tell any more lies. Christ, what did I say that to her for? What if she decides to find out? I don't know, perhaps she'll do a Google search for Patrick or contact another friend from university to find out. Though it doesn't sound like her husband gives her the freedom to run off onto social media. Yet, with what he's just done to her, the officers will have him in cuffs soon enough. Then Josie will have time on her hands; time she's never had before. She might decide to set up a Facebook alumni group and ask them if they know what happened to our ex-paramedic trainer.

My insides are screaming at me and I want to tear my hair clean out of my scalp as I walk back to the ambulance, outwardly a figure of composure and calmness.

I jump in the driver's seat. Despite Adele having had that duty on the way here, I'm hoping she'll get in the back with Josie without argument.

The back door of the ambulance opens and, thankfully, my partner is in the process of giving me exactly what I need: time on my own. My mind blocks their voices out. I've lied. I've lied again. This time to someone who could potentially find out quite easily.

Crashing through all my worries and fears, a harder and deeper voice takes over my thoughts: *So what? Who cares if Josie bloody Robertson finds out? Once you leave her at the hospital, you'll never have to see each other again. You did what you had to do.*

I did what I had to do.

Chapter sixteen

The wine is flowing tonight. Not usually something I do after work, mainly because I'm always so knackered and the thought of another heavy shift the following day sends me straight to bed. But this evening, it's called for. The two sides of my consciousness are battling with each other. The regret of lying versus the need to keep my secret safe, keep Rose safe.

I always intended on telling Rose the truth eventually, of course I did, so you mustn't think bad of me. You must understand it's hard to backtrack on a lie as huge as that. I could have said her father was a one-night stand, and I knew nothing about him and, when she was old enough to understand, I could have explained why I had said what I did, why I had lied to the crying face of my four-year-old daughter. To say the man was dead... that's something you can't come back from, whether she was thirteen, eighteen or twenty-one. I know it's something Rose would never understand. You can't just resurrect the dead – even the fictional dead. It doesn't work like that.

The Merlot is doing the trick. I don't hate myself as much as I did this afternoon. But my feelings are still raging. Now, however, they are aimed more towards Patrick. There he is, living like a lord in Brighton, with his *family*. Married. Settled. Happy. Ignorant to the lies I've told my daughter and my father and the few friends I have. I've shied away from anyone who wanted to get close to me, out of fear or guilt or shame. I'm not sure.

I'm glad he and Sadie have been living the last twenty years in marital bliss.

Ha, yeah, of course I am.

Why couldn't that have been me?

I can't help but picture him, as he was yesterday in that dimly lit pub, staring into my eyes like the past twenty years hadn't aged us, or changed us. His eyes are just as enticing, his skin is just as soft, and he still makes me want to rip his clothes off.

After everything he told me and despite him having everything I ever wanted, he still affects me as he always did.

Isn't it funny how people can do that to you? It doesn't matter if we love men or women, there's *always* someone – there's always that one person who can get away with so much in our lives. They can love us, control us, make us stand tall as well as crushing us. They have the power to change our moods in an instant, change the way we think and feel and, I suppose, completely change the course of our lives. But is it really them at all? Surely we've handed that power to them. We've allowed them to have an effect on our thoughts and feeling and ideas. So, actually, can't we take it back from them whenever we choose? Can't we decide when they no longer have the power?

Patrick is that person in my life, yet I still haven't taken the power back.

I nodded along to everything he said yesterday. Agreed with what he wanted and let *him* make *me* feel guilty for looking for Rose.

It became about protecting his *precious wife Sadie*, not Rose. How could I let that happen?

Why did I let that happen?

After all this time, am I really just going to trust Patrick again, no questions asked? The man who used me for years and dropped me over the cliff's edge without a second thought the moment Sadie gave him an ultimatum?

This isn't about them. It's about Rose; it's about my daughter. What if Rose has already uncovered my lie and that's the reason she isn't answering my calls and emails and messages?

The panic rises. A slow exhale trembles out of my mouth; a deep moan too, as if it's riding an invisible wave of heartache. Did I really think it would be impossible for her to find out the truth?

She's a young woman, hungry for a story, intent on someday putting pen to paper and writing a bestselling novel. What if the story I created all those years ago has been like fuel to the fire, inspiring her, and she's secretly been determined to find out who she really is and where she came from? You see those kinds of programmes on television all the time. Long-lost families and the like. Just because she thought her father was dead doesn't mean she wouldn't want to know his family – does she have any aunts and uncles and cousins and grandparents?

If that's the case… if it's possible and actually has happened…

She used to love telling her friends and teachers that she was a paramedic's daughter. Ha. As if she would be proud of me now. I would no longer be her hero – or anyone else's, for that matter. Rose could have found out what kind of a person I really am. A liar.

No, it can't be. Surely, my headstrong and fiery daughter wouldn't just ignore me if she had uncovered the mother of all fucking secrets like that. She would confront me. I know she would. Well, I think she would. University can change a person, can't it?

I'm pathetic. How could I just leave Brighton so easily yesterday without finding her? What, because *he* said it would be best for *his* family? What if that's actually Patrick's game? He intends on getting to her first and, in actual fact, he wants to break the news to Rose, tell her that her mother's lied her entire life. That way, he'll be the hero and I'll be… what will I be? I'll be the person who loses everything, that's who I'll be.

No. No fucking way. I can't let him do that.

I glance at the time. It's 10pm – too late to do much now. It took me a few moments to focus on the clock hands, and I realise the bottle of red is empty and the second one from the supermarket bag is on the table and open. I don't even remember opening that one. Before topping up my glass again, I grab my mobile phone and, with one eye closed to see the screen better, I compose a message to Dave.

I hope you don't mind the late text, but I don't think I'll be able to come in tomorrow.

Before the phone is out of my hand, Dave replies:

It's always nice to hear from you, Abi. Why? Hope you're okay, I'm here if you need anything.

Why? Good question.

Not feeling great… perhaps it's a delayed reaction to the situation on Friday.

I don't send that. I delete it. Dave will insist on counselling or something if I say that. My thumb dances over the phone as I retype my message:

I've been on the phone to my mum's carer at the hospice and she's not doing too great. She needs to see me. I think I need to spend some time with her.

It's not a complete lie. It did really happen, just a few days ago, and someone in my family does actually need me.

Oh, Abi, I'm so sorry to hear that. I hope your mum is okay. Take tomorrow as compassionate leave and we'll catch up tomorrow evening about the rest of your shifts for the week.
Thanks, Dave, feel awful to leave you in the lurch.
No worries, I can cover you – you helped me out today, so only fair.
Really appreciate it. Thanks again.
Speak tomorrow x

And it's done. I do feel awful, by the way; that part wasn't a lie. I know people rely on me. Hell, this city relies on the NHS like nowhere else in this country. The amount of emergency calls made every single day proves that. Yes, I'm a paramedic, but I'm a mother first and foremost. For now, I need to put those strangers to the back of my mind, and I need to make sure Patrick isn't swooping in and trying to be the hero.

First thing tomorrow morning, I'll be Brighton bound to end all of this. One way or another. It's my job to find Rose. It's my job to protect her from the truth. Patrick will not have the final say over my life this time. He will no longer have the power to do this to me.

No way in hell will I let my daughter find out about her father. No matter what I have to do.

Chapter seventeen

The weather isn't as off-putting as it was the last time I walked these streets in Brighton, thankfully. It's chilly, not wet, but to be honest with you I'm numb to most things right now, including the weather.

When I passed the student union building, I let my eyes roam over the windows, but I didn't stop. Not sure why. Even for a Tuesday morning there were a fair few bodies in there – the joys of uni life; I remember it well – but something kept telling me it wasn't where I'd find Rose. That's a laugh, really, because it's not like I can trust my mother's intuition at the moment. I'm completely off balance.

Another ten minutes and I'll be on Rose's road. I'm pretty sure she doesn't have any lectures this early; if I remember correctly it was one of the things that she loved about her timetable – mid-week lie-ins on Tuesdays and Wednesdays. Who wouldn't love that? The thought of Rose, who never wants to get out of bed, brings a smile to my face. She was the stereotypical teenager, always tucked away in her room. Even in the summer holidays, her curtains would be closed to block out the sun and she would sit in bed reading book after book. As a grown woman, she would need four different alarms on her phone, all pinging and beeping within a half an hour time period. Yes, she's a snoozer. It gives me a sliver of hope for this morning, that snuggled up in bed is exactly where I'll find my daughter.

Continuing along Edward Street, my eyes automatically dart to the left and scan the vicinity of John Street. I can't see any signs or obvious buildings, but I do know that's where Brighton Police Station is located. It gave me comfort to discover, when we moved

Rose down here, that in between the pubs and my daughter's residence there was a police presence. I'm not saying all students are youngsters who can't handle their booze but, in my line of work, you see it all too often: drunken bar fights, lovers' feuds that get way out of hand once fuelled with alcohol, freshers' week – no need to say any more on that one. Anyway, I've made a point of reminding myself where the police are. You know, just in case.

As I turn onto Rose's street, with the dull grey sea on the horizon, I notice her front door is open. My teeth beginning nibbling at the skin on my bottom lip. I stop and just observe the man exiting the property. I can't see who's on the other side of the door, who he's saying goodbye to. I wait until his back is to me before I cross the road. It all happened so quick, I only caught a brief glimpse of his face. Some stubble on his chin and cheeks, maybe – which instantly makes me think he's older than Rose – and a touch of grey to his dark hair. I can't be sure. He's off around the corner in a flash, his shoulders slumped and his hands tucked deep in his trouser pockets. He could well be older than Rose. How would I know? The ages of her housemates is something else I failed to ask. They are all female, or at least they were when Rose moved in. Penny is in her year… yes, I think I'm sure of that.

I knock on the front door and listen to footsteps banging around inside, and a voice asking, 'Did you forget something?' She obviously thinks it's her gentleman caller returned. It's not my Rose's voice.

'Oh, sorry, hi,' the girl says, taken aback by the stranger on her front doorstep. 'Yes, can I help you?'

I called her girl, but that's wrong, I shouldn't. She's clearly a woman. Not a woman of my maturity – easily mid-twenties, probably coming to the end of her studies. She's wearing a beautiful turquoise saree, adorned with beads and jewels, but it's not wrapped to perfection around her body – her jet-black hair is somewhat dishevelled looking too. It's a beautiful outfit nonetheless. She catches me taking in her appearance and tries to smooth down the wild strands while adjusting the beaded material simultaneously.

'I'm really in quite a rush… family occasion,' she says, and fans a hand along her body, as if to explain the saree. I wouldn't explain the choice of outfit if I were her. They are so exquisitely tailored, I'd happily wear one every day if I wasn't a paramedic. It would probably cause problems with all the blood and people-carrying. 'Whatever it is you're selling, I'm afraid–'

I raise a hand and stop the petite Indian woman in her tracks. 'Not selling a thing. I'm just a mother surprising her daughter.' She frowns, probably at my squeaky voice and fake smile. 'Sorry for being so cryptic,' I continue. 'I'm Rose's mother.'

I stop myself from adding, 'I'm here to take her to breakfast' and blah blah blah. I don't owe this person any kind of explanation. *Just let me over the threshold for crying out loud.* I feel as if I should be flashing some kind of ID.

'Oh, sorry, I didn't realise. Rose didn't mention anything.' She finally backs away from the door and lets me in. She doesn't move too far into the corridor and I feel like I'm invading her space. 'I'm Sheetal, by the way.'

'Hi, I'm Abi.' My hand thrusts itself to her automatically. Her limp handshake intensifies the awkwardness. I guess students aren't hand-shakers any more… who knew? 'So, is Rose upstairs or…'

Sheetal frowns again. 'I wouldn't know. I haven't seen her since before the weekend. That's what I mean. Strange she didn't say you were coming, cos I'm pretty sure she's not here.'

My heart sinks. I think I mumble some kind of reply, a weak *oh* sound. I'm unsure of what else to say – except demanding she give me proof. My stomach squirms.

'Well, surely Rose could be in her room, Sheetal. You don't live out of each other's pockets, do you?'

She fiddles with the waistband of her saree, straightening it up again. 'Well, no, of course we don't. I just mean I know I've been alone all morning.'

'Except for the man who left just before I knocked.' There's a harshness in my tone that can't be ignored, and I point to the door over my shoulder in a stabbing manner. The intention isn't to sound like a bitchy detective; yet, it somehow manages to come across that way.

'I… err… oh yeah,' Sheetal stutters and won't make eye contact with me. 'That was just… a friend. Our friend.'

'Our friend?' I echo. 'As in yours and Rose's?' Okay, I'm nailing the detective questioning now, but it's her fault. She sounds all nervous and insincere, nothing like she did just moments before.

'Yeah, like, we all know him.' She glances at me briefly. 'Listen, as I said, there's no one here and I really have to get going.'

I pull my arms up and cross them over my chest. Something is really bugging me here. 'That wasn't Dylan leaving by any chance, was it?'

Sheetal gasps a laugh – I think it's a laugh – but shakes her head. 'No, that wasn't Dylan. Like I said, just a friend, and I really have to–'

'Get going, yes, you've said. Well, I'm not stopping you.'

She trips over her words again. 'D-d-did you want to leave Rose a message?'

'No, no. I won't hold you up any more, you head off. I'll wait in my daughter's room.'

The woman's frown deepens. 'But I don't know when she'll be back. I can't just let you hang out in there.'

It's my turn to mirror the facial expression. 'You can't? I'm afraid you have no say in the matter, Sheetal. I'm going up to my daughter's room, where I'll wait for her for as long as I see fit.' Wow, I've never adopted such a headmistress tone of voice before; I almost feel sorry for the woman as I reign my new power over the house. 'If you have a problem with that, I suggest you call the police.'

Sheetal's head jerks back as if I've raised a fist to her. I want to laugh at all of this. What possessed me to say that? Why in God's name would she call the police? My daughter lives here.

Her shock disappears, and I wonder if I went in a little too hard. Sheetal puffs out her cheeks and blows hot air in my direction, as if to say 'whatever, lady'. If only she knew how I was feeling, then she would understand why my mood is so changeable. Actually, in all honesty, she probably wouldn't – no one else seems to.

She's definitely given up on me, and she shrugs her slender shoulders while saying, 'Do as you like, Mrs Quinn. I'm really not that fussed.'

I go to correct her on the Mrs title, but what's the point? She doesn't seem tetchy any more, or worried by my questions. She looks bored of me. Yet she still stands there in front of me, not allowing me to pass, and the lack of urgency makes me want to click my fingers in her face.

'Didn't you say you had a family wedding or something to get to, Sheetal?' I manage, without the impatient hand action.

The doubt is in her eyes again; they're shifty and roaming around the house. Doesn't she want me to be here alone?

'Err… yes, shortly. My dad is collecting me. Rose's room is upstairs… first on the right.'

'I remember.' My giant step towards the stairs leaves Sheetal no choice but to shift out of my way. We brush shoulders. 'Enjoy your family event,' I say, before climbing up to my daughter's bedroom.

* * *

I haven't moved from the same spot on my daughter's bed for over an hour and a half. Sheetal's footsteps pitter-pattered past the bedroom door a few times, even lingering outside for a few seconds. She never knocked or called out. Not even after a car horn honked outside, or before the front door opened and banged shut. Then I heard nothing more; the housemate had left for her family occasion, or whatever she'd said.

I've been alert since then, hoping to hear the sound of the door go again, so I could welcome Rose home.

But it's been dead silent.

I let my eyes wonder around Rose's room. Again. It's so neat and tidy, everything in its place. Just the way she likes it. We've always joked that she's Monica from the TV programme *Friends*. She's been that way since she was a young girl. Nothing seems out of place, but how would I know really? After Rose moved in, I only saw the inside of this house, and her bedroom, one other time. If I ever did venture to Brighton – which wasn't often, as Rose preferred to visit home, she said – we always met up at the station and went shopping or for lunch. I did notice her bed is neatly made, and considering the early hour in which I travelled down here, I can only assume Rose started her day just as early and is studying in the library.

Or she didn't stay here at all last night.

I hate all this second-guessing. The not knowing. It's driving me insane; I'm creating images and stories in my mind. You know the ones: son or daughter doesn't answer the phone and it's because they've drowned at the nearby beach; son or daughter doesn't reply to your message and it's because they've been beaten to death by a scumbag after their wallet or purse. Understand this: these images aren't just coming from a neurotic mother who's being ignored by her child, but also from a paramedic who's come across some nasty things over the years.

The urge to go through drawers and wardrobes and read letters and notepads is overwhelming. Something is stopping me. I'm not sure what. Perhaps my consciousness has woken up and is telling me I've done enough shitty things – especially to Rose. I need to know if she is here somewhere – on campus, at the library or in a lecture – or if she didn't stay here at all. I need to hunt down this Dylan guy.

My hand slips down to the bedside table and pulls open the top drawer. I close my eyes and sigh. Snooping is never a good idea.

I reach in and pull out Rose's mobile. Why doesn't she have it with her? This is probably an old one. Her phone contract has been upgraded since being in Brighton, surely?

After a few tries of the power button, it's clear the phone is dead. That answers that, then. It is an old phone and she's keeping it as a backup. Ever the logical one is my Rose.

As if it's burnt my hand, I chuck the phone back in its place and slam the drawer shut. I stand up, drawn to the corkboard leaning against the wall on top of her desk – this isn't prying, because whatever's on it is there for all to see. Granted, she probably wasn't expecting her mother to visit. There are a few photos. No faces I really recognise. Some look familiar. I'm guessing it's because I've seen these photos or people on Rose's Facebook page. There's also a lecture timetable. Tuesdays are empty. A huge free day for Rose to do as she wishes: study, sleep, socialise, shop. To do anything. Be anywhere. Her first lecture tomorrow isn't until noon, and suddenly I feel like an idiot being in her room.

What was I expecting? That I'd hole up in here until… until when, exactly? I have no idea what my daughter is doing or where she is.

Everything is glaring at me: the wardrobe, the chest of drawers, the laptop. It's as if they're daring me, tempting me to rifle through them all and… and what? Find the answers I'm looking for?

Instead, I grab my mobile from my handbag and call Rose's number again. It doesn't ring – straight to voicemail. The indecision of what to do is burning my chest as if I'm stuck in a desert storm, choking on the air around me and unable to see anything clearly. This room is suffocating, and I turn for the door. But before I run from my daughter's room and straight out the front door, something inside makes me backtrack, yank open the top drawer again and snatch up Rose's iPhone.

Chapter eighteen

The breeze does nothing to shake away the dazed feeling clouding my mind. I retrace my steps towards the train station, despite knowing one thing: I can't go back to London. The way I feel, I couldn't care less who wants to call me dramatic, or even too involved in my grown daughter's life. I need to see Rose.

At John Street, I stop walking. Like a statue on the kerb, I'm stood staring down the road, directly at the building where the police station is located. What would I tell them? I can see it now: some young officer telling me that Rose is an adult, and with no evidence of foul play, there is little they can do. I've met enough coppers over the years to know how it works.

I've never felt such indecision. The tears trickle down my cheeks, slow and quiet, and I feel like a fool. An idiot for standing here, frustrated and alone, not knowing what to do. I'm a grown woman who makes fast and snap decisions to save people's lives. Why am I finding it so hard to decide what's best here? I wipe my cheeks, breathe deep and gaze around the tranquil beachside street. That's when I see him. On the opposite side of the road, walking towards me, his face still burrowed into the collar of his dark leather jacket, is the guy I watched leave Rose's house moments before I knocked on the door.

In a flash, I decide to follow him; funny how that bolt of an idea came quickly enough. I watch too many crime programmes.

Before I can conceal myself, so he doesn't notice me, he jumps into the passenger seat of a silver Vauxhall Corsa. It's parked facing away from me, therefore I can't see him or the person in the driver's seat. The engine doesn't rumble to life. There's no movement from the vehicle, and my feet are put to work again.

I walk slowly, my focus never leaving the Corsa, my back practically sliding along the red-brick wall to my right. The need to see what's happening is powering me forward. What if Rose is the driver? When I reach eye-level with the front of the car, I take my phone out of my pocket and pretend to be busy looking at the map, turning slightly to catch a sly look at the people inside it.

It's Patrick.

Even with just a peeping side glance at the man, I know it's him. If I had not seen him the other day, I would have thought my mind was playing tricks on me. Now I know he's here, I couldn't be surer of anything else – or anyone else. That is one hundred per cent Patrick in the driver's seat. Why the hell is he in a car with the man who just left Rose's house?

I cross the road. Despite having no clue what my next action will be, my brain seems to have a line of communication with my body that I'm unaware of. Just as I creep up to the back of the car, the passenger door swings open. The mystery man steps out and slams it shut behind him. Puffs of smoke blow from the exhaust as the engine starts, and my feet are at it again. Suddenly, I'm yanking open the door and sliding myself into the seat which had just been vacated.

'What the f–' Patrick begins, stopping short when he sees my face. 'Abi.'

'What's going on?' I demand. It would appear that automatic line of communication from my brain is also connected to my mouth. I'm doing and saying things without even needing to think of them. So much for the tearful mother stuck on the street corner just minutes earlier. 'What the hell are you playing at, Patrick?'

'What do you mean? What are you doing here?' he retaliates, and I hear my own accusatory tone mirrored in his.

'Who was that guy just now? I saw him leave Rose's house earlier and now here he is chatting to you. Don't deny it. Is he some private investigator?'

I have no idea where that came from, and my question throws Patrick as much as it does me. He frowns, and a look of confusion spreads across his face. But there's more. He hasn't shaved since the last time I saw him, and the dark hairy stubble stains his face. He's wearing the same outfit too. Men can usually get away with buying the same jeans and jumpers and wearing only one coat – therefore always looking the same – but this is different. Patrick looks unkempt. Even the red rim around his eyes makes me think he hasn't slept for days. Perhaps my revelation about Rose hit him harder than I gave him credit for; he has a secret daughter out there, living so close to him and his family, yet we've no idea where she is.

'Are you okay?' I soften. It could have been my tone, but tears spring into his eyes, and I instinctively reach for his hand. 'Patrick.'

'Abi, I wasn't honest with you the other day.'

I'm frozen, except for the hot rush of blood coursing through my veins. 'W-what do you mean?'

'When you told me about Rose, I lied. I know who she is. My stupid fault for not connecting the Quinn surname. To be honest, I didn't even think of it as your surname too.'

What a slap in the face. I say nothing, too scared to stop Patrick mid-flow when he's telling the truth… yet I'm also too scared to hear any more. I allow him to continue anyway.

'When I saw you, it was obvious. I knew you were her mother straight away. Not just the surname, but your face, your beautiful porcelain skin, your chestnut eyes with flecks of green, and the hair…'

'Don't tell me about my hair. Get on with it.'

'Rose is your freaking double, Abi. Just how you looked in Scotland in your twenties.'

Patrick's eyes are filled with dark shadows and tears. I shudder, like someone's walked over my grave – another old saying courtesy of Mum. He clears his throat before saying, 'I know Rose. And that man you just saw leave the car is my son. His name is Dylan and he's—'

I gasp and look away, causing Patrick to stop talking. There's no need for him to explain who Dylan is. In my head, despite the muffle of the voicemail, I can hear Rose's voice saying that Dylan knew. The man I've wondered about, over and over again… Patrick's sleepless, red eyes tell me everything I need to know.

'The person Rose is dating.' I finish his sentence, but the emotional blockage in my throat catches and sounds more like a banshee's wail.

Patrick nods in my peripheral vision and he grabs my fingers before my hand slides away.

'There's more, isn't there?' I whisper.

I can feel it: in the way he's touching me, in the way his chest hitches with every breath he takes. He continues to nod. My stomach clenches as my thoughts turn to the worst. Rose is pregnant; the reason I can't find Rose is because she's in the process of moving in with Dylan; Rose and Dylan are engaged.

But it can't be any of those things because they are huge scenarios in my daughter's life. Jesus Christ, we haven't had an argument to explain why she wouldn't have told me any of this. I'm her mother and she knows that she can confide in me no matter what.

Unless…

Her voicemail said, 'Dylan knows', but what if I misheard her? What if she was telling me that she and Dylan know? What if the two of them discovered the truth about me and Patrick all those years ago? They know they're not just boyfriend and girlfriend, but also half-brother and half-sister. I choke on the stuffy air, heaving and retching.

I turn to Patrick, needing to hear what he knows before I pass out from the torturous thoughts swirling in my mind.

He inhales deeply, his chin quivering as he says, 'I had an affair… with… with my son's girlfriend.'

Chapter nineteen

The words spin and crash against my skull like the waves raging towards the sand.

I pull my hand from Patrick's and face the few strangers walking along the street as they prepare for university and work and normal everyday life.

Patrick's son is Dylan.

Dylan's girlfriend is Rose.

Patrick had sex with Dylan's girlfriend.

'Abi, say something. I've felt terrible. That's why no one can know. My mind is wild at the moment, but you have to understand–'

My right hand swings round and strikes Patrick in the face with so much force he yelps, and a trickle of blood soon begins to drip from his nostril.

His voice. His face.

How dare he speak.

The air is completely sucked from the car and I gasp for breath. My storming head is dizzy, the light-headedness threatening to take over. I can't pass out. I can't be in here.

I reach for the door and, although I feel as if I haven't an ounce of strength left in my body, I push it open and climb out. Patrick's voice lingers in the background, calling my name, and I hear his door open too. I can't be near him.

I set off, back towards Rose's house at a pace I didn't know I could reach. Running from a monster, I dash along the road, not stopping to even check if a car is coming or if Patrick is following me. I gain momentum and I'm charging towards the seafront, my legs carrying me away from the car, from him, from the worst thing I could have ever been told.

Finally, I collapse on to my knees in the cold seaside sand, and the vomit which had gradually been building finally erupts from my body. My eyes water, my nose runs, and I scream. Not a blood-curdling cry of fear, but a painful howl of fury.

Who am I mad at? Who deserves my anger?

I've run away from Patrick the monster, but is it really just him?

Me. I'm a monster too.

No! I'm bloody not. I'm neither a monster nor a liar. I am a mother, willing to do whatever needs to be done to shield her child from pain. To protect her from the truth of knowing she was never wanted by her father. Rose has never needed to know that she was conceived out of some obsessive, sordid affair. No one would want to discover that's where they came from.

I half-stand and stumble away from the stench of my own puke, my unsteady legs bringing me closer to the water's edge, and I plonk down, facing the sea.

What have I done?

It would be so easy to hate Patrick. To place the blame clearly with him. But how can I? How can I truly blame a man for sleeping with a woman he didn't know was his daughter?

Because he's married.

Because she's his son's girlfriend.

My stomach lurches again at the thought of Dylan. The thought of Rose with Dylan. And then the thought of Rose with Patrick.

The bile swirls in my mouth and I have no choice but to open my lips and let it dribble to the sand again, this time mixed with tears and snot that I have no control over.

I gaze out to the sea, my vision blurry, still unable to ignore the grey-and-white breakers rolling around. Each wave is crashing into the next. They're unable to stop themselves, for it's the way of life… just like with people. The course of the water changes on a daily basis, hourly even, and the tide cannot know where it will strike next or what natural disaster will disrupt its flow and transform it into a tsunami or tidal wave, ready to take apart people's worlds bit by bit.

Just like I've done.

I wonder how far I could walk out into the water before it would lift me and carry me out with it, consume me and end me.

I shed my coat and handbag and allow my legs to lift me up, allow my feet to begin their journey towards the sea. It's not until I'm standing with the water waist high, the waves knocking against my chest, that I realise the selfishness of my actions.

With the tide going out, it takes all my energy to push against the water and walk back to the beach. By time I flop down on to the sand again, my legs have given up on me completely. With my face so close to the itchy grains, I spot a shimmer of a jewel near my coat. My fingers reach out, dip into the wet sand, and pull out a gorgeous heart-shaped ruby with a broken silver clasp. It could belong to anyone. I'm sure jewellery and all sorts are lost daily on this beach, but it doesn't belong to just anyone. I know that.

The reason I know is because this stunning charm belongs to Rose.

I run my finger along the very small chip at the point of the heart – small enough that a stranger would never notice it – and release a strangled cry. A family heirloom given to my mother when she was pregnant with me, by her sister, who sadly had no children before she passed away. Then it was given to me when I gave birth to Rose, and finally passed down to my daughter when she left for university last year – so she always had a piece of me with her. The very small blemish to the ruby happened many years ago, my mother once told me, when her sister Nora took part in a mass protest rally in London in the sixties. Nora, an anti-war and anti-bomb activist, was given the precious stone by her childhood sweetheart and fiancé – who died during active duty – and the clasp had broken during the protest, smashing to the ground and slightly chipping the heart's point. My mother always said Nora never had it fixed because it reminded her of something special: the day she stood up and had her say for what she believed in.

The thought of Nora's bravery is shadowed by the idea of Rose being here, at the entrance to the sea, and contemplating the worst. It whacks me with a heaviness I can barely take. I peer over my shoulder at the raging tide and wonder if Rose found the strength to walk back out of the water, like I did – if she ever entered it at all.

I'm so confused. I'm so lost. My brain feels like a dog's squeaky toy.

Squeak.

The noise interrupts me again and again.

Squeak. Squeak.

I turn back to be greeted by morning beach walkers with their dogs – that explains the noise – and eager tourists, all of whom are beginning to peer my way. Fuck me, what a mess I must look to them. Before a Good Samaritan comes my way, I heave myself up and walk – well, stomp is a nearer likeness to what I'm doing – to the street. Hopefully everyone thinks I'm a student who had too much to drink last night and decides to ignore me.

From my place on the promenade, the line of B&Bs become a dozen beacons in front of me. I draw the air deep into my lungs, pulling my chest and shoulders up, and straighten my back. My only thoughts now are of my daughter.

Could I really believe it was okay to walk out into the sea and end my own life, when Rose's is in complete turmoil? Does she even know the truth? What if she stood here, having the exact same contemplations, thinking of ending her life because… because what? I can't be sure, because I don't know what my daughter flaming well knows at this point.

She needs her mother.

With more vengeance than I've ever had before, as if the sea actually knocked some sense into me, I know exactly what needs to be done, and exactly who needs to be focused on. I stride towards the nearest townhouse with a vacancy sign in the window.

With renewed vigour, I finally understand why Patrick wanted to keep his knowledge of Rose a secret. But the real question is: how far is he willing to go to make sure that happens?

Chapter twenty

Rose stood on the beach with tears streaming down her face. She gave a guttural groan of pain every now and then between silent sobs. Facing the sea, with just the full moon as a guiding light, it was difficult to determine how far out the tide really was. She could hear the waves lapping against each other, but the noise was quiet and gentle. Tranquil even.

She didn't know how long she had been standing there in the pitch blackness of the night. She paid no attention to the goosebumps growing along her pale skin. She had no care for the chill whipping around her – actually, she embraced it. The fact that she could feel the cold meant she could still feel *something*.

Her mind felt as empty as her body, and Rose couldn't help but wonder how far she would have to walk out before she felt the tip of the water's edge on her feet. How long would it take for the tide to snake along her bare legs, saturate her skirt with its salty water and taint her body?

Tainted. Again.

Just like that, her thoughts flew from the simplicity of the sea and the moon back to Patrick Malone. Rose shuddered at the memory of the last few hours: at the decision she had made to visit Patrick in his office on campus; at allowing her lustful temptations to take her away from a loving boyfriend to his monster of a father; at the way his hand crawled along her thigh; at the way she had told him to stop.

Did she say it loud enough? Rose questioned herself. Did she shout *no* loud enough so that Patrick understood? Was changing your mind that late in the game allowed? If she went to him with those feelings of lust and playing with the idea of sex, was it actually too late to say stop?

The questions of doubt and uncertainty swam around her mind like the endless shadow of the sea in front of her. Did she really doubt herself at all? Rose wrapped her arms around herself, deciding she needed some warmth in her bones, and briefly thought of her mother.

Rose was the paramedic's daughter, a title she loved to share with people, and had been taught about different dangers from a young age. All the accidents, the tragedies, the crimes her mother had faced were explained to her, so Rose's eyes were open to the wrongs and rights of the world.

Deep in her heart, she knew. She knew that as much as she had been tempted by her boyfriend's father, as much as she thought she wanted something to happen with him, she had said no. Rose told Patrick to stop touching her and he ignored her pleas. He continued to lift her skirt. He continued to drop his trousers. He continued to force himself inside of her, unprotected. She had said no.

The tears came thick and fast; the darkness around her had nothing to do with why she could no longer see. She tried to wipe them away, but more travelled down her cheeks as quickly as she cleared the path.

'I thought I'd find you here, you whore.'

The violent words were hissed in her ear from behind. Rose spun around and gasped.

'W-what are you doing here?'

'I could ask you the same question,' Dylan shouted as he stomped towards her.

The lamp posts behind him blinded her momentarily. As her eyes adjusted to the brightness, she didn't see his hand coming towards her. But she felt his whack across the side of her head, forcing her to crash down on to the shore.

'Did you really think I wouldn't find out?' He continued his verbal abuse while gripping Rose's wrist and dragging her back up from the sand like a rag doll. 'Did you really think you would get away with… with *that*?'

Stunned, she was unable to reply. Not that Dylan seemed at all interested in allowing her to answer his questions as he tightened his grip around her and hauled Rose towards the sea.

Chapter twenty-one

I've slept the afternoon away. I'm not entirely sure how, what with the fuzz that continually clouds my brain, but somehow, after I showered and regained some warmth in my body, I conked out on the single bed by the window.

The hotel room is a basic one. I'm not bothered, as it's all I need. The bath towel is still wrapped around me, because my clothes and boots are drying on the two small radiators on either side of the bedroom. As the night-time sky casts its dimness into the room, I flick the switch on the lamp – not that it adds much light – and gaze out of the window.

My chest feels heavy as I watch the people below on the prom go about their business. How lucky are they to wander freely around the seaside, perhaps debating where to go for dinner or which book to read tonight? I, on the other hand, am nowhere near the comfort of my own home and have no idea what my family are thinking or doing or what they'll eat tonight. That's not why the heaviness inside me continues to weigh me down though.

Shaking myself from my thoughts, I grab my handbag from the floor and take out my phone; there isn't a lot of battery life and I didn't bring a charger. I must remember to pop into a shop at some point this evening.

I don't know how long I'm staying here. I haven't thought about that. I've paid for one night. Hopefully that's all it will take.

No messages or missed calls from Rose. There is one from Dave, asking how I am and how my mother is.

Why is he asking after Mum?

Oh shit, of course, because that's the reason I took the day off. To visit Mum. I really must call the hospice. Instead I compose a reply to Dave, telling him I need tomorrow off too. I can't think about work right now, which is totally unheard of for me. The thought of concentrating on strangers, on rescuing them and their families, makes my stomach somersault. I need to concentrate on my own; on my daughter.

The only way I can do that is to find Patrick. My time wallowing in the sea came with a spark of clarity that Patrick is the key to finding Rose. I saw his face in the car, before he delivered the bombshell.

The bile rises in my mouth again. I push it down. There's no time for my feelings.

I just know there was more to what he said, that there's more going on. When I think about Patrick's son, about Dylan, and the way he carried himself in the street this morning, he looked… cagey. As if he were trying to slink around. Leaving Rose's place in the early morning with his head bowed low, then sloping into his father's car nearly two hours later, but still close to the house. Where had he gone while I was in Rose's bedroom?

Also, I can't help thinking there was something off about the way he exited Patrick's car. He was no longer slouched and slow. There was more of a temper about his actions: whacking the car door shut and practically sprinting off down the street. What had Patrick and his son spoken about so briefly?

'Dylan knows.'

'Dylan knows.'

Rose's voice echoes in my mind. It's the only part of the voicemail that stands out. I swipe my finger across my phone's screen, bringing up the voicemail options, and listen to my daughter's voice again. It's pointless. There are only snippets repeating themselves.

'Mum, are you okay…? I'm–'

'It was Penny's idea and… I'm sorry… Dylan knows.'

What is Rose saying sorry for. And what in heaven's name does Dylan know?

The only way to find out is to ask him himself, I decide. But if I can't even find my own daughter, how the hell will I find her bo—

No, I can't call him that. He's not her boyfriend.

My throat is dry. Only for a few minutes, mind you, as the bitter fluid returns, rising up my throat and swamping my mouth. With no other choice available, I dash to the bathroom and empty the contents of my stomach in the sink. I have nothing left to give, and my body jerks with empty promises of vomit.

For a split second, I'm floored by my thoughts, by my weakness and by my inability to answer any of my own questions. But then I see the ruby jewel on the chest of drawers to the side of me and I march back into the bedroom and snatch it up. Enclosing it in my fist, I refuse to drop to my knees and give in.

* * *

Thirty minutes later, wearing damp clothes – but resembling some kind of sane person – I've left the B&B and am pounding the pavement towards Rose's house. I have no intention of knocking on her front door again. I just *know* she isn't there. Instead, my focus is on Patrick. He has the answers to cleaning up this godawful mess. If he refuses to tell me where Rose is, then at least he can lead me to his son, because something is telling me, with one hundred per cent certainty, that one of those men knows where my daughter is.

The sea breeze is heaven-sent. Not that it's doing anything to clear my mind's haze, but it is spurring me on as I take the turn onto Rose's road. I edge closer to the town centre, to the train station and the student union and that dingy pub where Patrick took me a few days ago, when, although my daughter was still missing, life felt simpler. The quaint public house is my destination. If Patrick isn't there, I'll ask after him. If I have no luck, I'll head to the university. I'm sure to get some locations or hints of his whereabouts. I may even be able to find out his address or discover exactly where the building he teaches in is. Granted, there's sure to be no lectures happening at this time – the night has completely taken over even though it's six in the evening – but I won't leave until I have some concrete information.

My spirit is lifted, only slightly but lifted nonetheless, at having a purpose. A mission.

With my aunt Nora's ruby heart gem safely tucked inside my jean pocket, I attempt to channel her bravery. It's soon knocked with the weight of a thousand punches when I spy two people ahead of me, standing on the pavement outside Rose's house.

I cross the road, but keep advancing, using the shadows to conceal me and stay away from the light shining from the lamp posts. As I approach, I make out the glistering sequins of the saree I saw Sheetal wearing earlier today. The person she's talking to has their back to me. I know who it is and can't help feeling fear and anger and apprehension all at once.

Patrick's hand is locked around Sheetal's wrist and she's obviously trying to pull away from him. I'm too far away to see if she's crying; it's hard to ignore the look of panic on her face. There are mumbled voices, but the wind takes their words away on the breeze and I have no idea what they're saying. I fear if I get any closer, one of them will spot me, and I don't want them to know I'm here. Edging a little closer, as close as I dare, I crouch behind a black Range Rover parked on the kerb and use it to shield me.

My heart is racing as Patrick points a long white finger at a scared looking Sheetal. What could he be saying to her to entice such a frightened look onto her petite face? He towers above her small frame; is that not enough dominance for him?

And then he's off, powering down the road away from Sheetal and away from me. I can't see his car anywhere, and he doesn't seem to be slowing down. He launches down the street with giant steps, each footstep thundering against the pavement like he's the Hulk.

I know I should wait until he's out of sight. What if he turns back and catches me? My mind reacts before my body can tell it to stop and I'm legging it across the road, catching Sheetal before she enters the house.

'Are you okay?' I call out as she rummages through her sequinned clutch bag, obviously looking for her keys.

The poor girl is trembling – how else wouldn't she have found the keys in such a small space? Sheetal looks at me, but seems to look straight through me, as if she doesn't recognise me.

'It's Abi, remember? We met this morning. I'm Rose's mum.'

She nods her head, though there still doesn't seem to be any recognition from her, and I can't help noticing the welling of tears in her eyes.

'I… I can't t-talk,' Sheetal stutters. 'I'm sorry.'

The keys appear in her hand. I'm losing her.

'That man. The one you were just talking to–'

'Mr… Mr Malone?'

'Yes, the university lecturer,' I say, playing along with her. 'Did he upset you?'

Sheetal's chin quivers, and I do feel a slight sadness for her, but I really don't have time to pander to her sorrow. Not when I have to find my daughter.

'No, no, he was just looking for… for his son. Dylan. I share a class with him.'

'Did he ask you about Rose?'

She frowns and slowly shakes her head. A single tear escapes and runs down her brown skin. 'N-n-no.'

She's lying. This is pointless.

I gaze up the street, in the direction Patrick walked off in. I can't be sure, as the darkness of the evening is doing its best to hide him in the shadows, but it looks as though he takes a left at the bottom of the road. That would lead to the pub we visited. I don't know the area. Not for sure. There are probably another dozen destinations he could be travelling to by taking that route.

I turn back to Sheetal. Her stunned face reminds me of a deer stuck in headlights, and I realise I'm not going to get much from her. Patrick obviously has some hold over her too.

'Did Mr Malone tell you where he might look for Dylan next? Did he say where he was going?'

For a moment, it feels like she's about to reveal everything to me: why she's on the verge of shedding a waterfall of tears, what Patrick said and why he has a hold over her. She doesn't. A shrug and down-turned lips are the only answers I receive.

'I really need to find Rose.'

I stop, hearing the tremble in my own voice, the desperation in it that makes it hard for me to breathe, to concentrate. I just want some help from someone – from the only person I've spoken to in Brighton who knows Rose – yet I know there's a reason this woman is holding something back from me. Why? That's an entirely different conundrum altogether. Is it Patrick? Could he really be doing this? Talking to Rose's friends and housemates, getting there before me, instructing them not to talk to Rose's crazed mother?

My words don't seem to have an effect on Sheetal. I can only hope that she sympathises with my pain, and that she recognises the look of sadness on my face – the same look I see etched on hers.

'Do you know where Rose is?' The air catches in my throat again, so I pause to clear it and attempt to smile. 'Please, if you know anything – where she's gone or who she's with – you would really be helping a mum out here.'

That burning desire of optimism flashes once more in my heart; the feeling that Sheetal is about to show some compassion. I'm wrong again, because she simply shakes her head, takes a deep breath and says, 'I'm sorry. I can't tell you anything.'

Chapter twenty-two

A voice in my head shouts at me, making my body jerk, and I dash away from Sheetal. She was never going to help me; Patrick is definitely manipulating her, just like he once used to do to me. With his older-man good looks and professor charm, and that Scottish sing-song voice of his, he's a hard man to resist. Who was I kidding, thinking I could cry like a baby and expect help from Sheetal? She's not a mother; she can't understand.

That man is a monster. A monster who continues to taint young women, including my daughter Rose... *his* d–

No, I can't even think it.

That thought conjures a picture in my mind that... that truly makes me retch.

How could he do this, the nasty piece of twisted shit?

How could he do this to my Rose?

I'm forced to slow my pace. Not unsurprising, really, since I'm running on empty. Empty except for the vile thoughts swirling inside me.

Bending over and resting my hands on my thighs to catch my breath is a big mistake. It's as if my body has taken this action as a sign and that I'm saying it's okay to vomit all over the pavement. Thankfully, I don't. What could I throw up? I can't remember the last time I ate or drank anything. Funny how life's necessities take a back seat when your loved ones are in danger. Our bodies just automatically know how to respond: *no, we no longer need fuel to survive, and we will plough on with our mission, regardless of exhaustion and dehydration.*

I lean back against the wooden fence of a house behind me and ask myself what I should do. What would my mum do, or what would my aunt Nora have done if she was in this position? Patrick is long gone. I never should have stopped to talk to Sheetal. He was the key to me finding Rose; I should have stayed with him. Okay, there's that pub a little farther on that I could check out, like I had planned all along, but other than that I have nothing. If he's not there, and part of me highly doubts he will be since he seems to be on his own mission to throw me off the scent, I have no clue where else he would be.

Street lamps ping on in a timely fashion around the bustling and busy square to my left. The chill has picked up and large puffs of white air escape my lips each time I exhale. It's fucking freezing. And so dark. It feels more like midnight than early evening. Stuffing my hands into my pockets, I feel the ruby heart in my right hand and clamp my fingers around it tightly.

What should I do? Where do I go from here?

I gaze along the quiet street. Do I walk in the direction Patrick went? There definitely seems to be more life there: traffic, busy shops open for business and pedestrians zig-zagging in and out of each other. I glance back down the road to Rose's house: shadows, silence and the unknown. I shudder and look away, catching the road sign directly opposite me as I do: John Street.

Somehow, I've managed to bring myself full circle and I'm stood right where I need to be. How could I have been so slow and stupid? This is what I should have done days ago, and if not then, certainly when I found out what a monster Patrick is. Releasing the gemstone from my grip, my arms begin to swing full force like I'm an army sergeant, and I power on towards Brighton's police station.

Chapter twenty-three

It took about twenty minutes, but the young officer at the reception desk finally realised I was going nowhere until I had spoken to someone in charge. It's amazing, really, the different reaction you receive when you give someone the stern don't-fuck-with-this-mother look rather than the desperate I'm-about-to-cry-and-this-mummy-needs-help look.

Now I'm in some kind of family room, I guess – it's probably not called that at all, but it's definitely not the dark and dingy interview rooms I've seen on TV – with an aging, balding and slightly large officer. Granted, I haven't painted a picture of Tom Hardy in a uniform, but there's something about this guy that is warm and cuddly, rather than austere and uninviting. I decide to appeal to his better nature. Praise be to God that he actually has one.

'Before you say anything, Officer…'

'Bellamy.'

'Officer Bellamy. I know how this may sound. My friends and colleagues have warned me that I'm totally overreacting, and you'll probably think this is a waste of your time. But, you see, I work in the emergency services too. I'm a paramedic and I've seen my fair share of tragedies and accidents, even murders and suicides. So please understand, I'm not here on some kind of whim. I truly need your help.'

I've got him. He's warmed to my words. I can see it just in the way he slouches his shoulders slightly – not in a bored way, but in a 'okay, I'm listening' kind of way. His clenched jaw loosens. I've piqued his interest, and before I lose it, I regurgitate everything that's happened in my life – sort of like a child at Christmas, giving Santa their never-ending list of wants and needs – since Rose called me on the day of the terrorist attack. For some reason, I skirt around the subject of Patrick Malone. It isn't a conscious decision, and not something I pre-determined but, as I tell Officer Bellamy about Rose going missing, it becomes apparent the kind of shitstorm that could hit if I tell him about Patrick. The man I had an affair with, who is Rose's father, isn't actually dead like I have had her believe her entire life but is alive and well in Brighton and now having an affair with his son's girlfriend and ultimately his daughter.

No, that's not something I can just casually drop into my statement. I'm actually pleased my mind automatically skipped that part of this awful nightmare, because I'm sure my tears and involuntary retching would not have held me in good stead for help and support from the police. Officer Bellamy probably would have ended this chat immediately and had me carted off to the nearest psych unit.

No, this is solely about finding Rose. Once that happens, who knows? But as long as she's found first, that's my main concern.

'Okay, Ms Quinn–'

'Please, call me Abi.' I hear the quiver in my own voice, catch the withering expression on Officer Bellamy's face, and I can guess where he's going.

He nods. Turns down his lips in some kind of fake I'm-an-understanding-person smile. It hits me then that I've probably shown that face to so many patients and their families over the years. God, it's patronising.

'As you wish, Abi. I have to be honest with you, this is difficult. Because of your daughter's age, we have to assume she can take care of herself until there's a good reason to think otherwise. So, the fact that you've already been to her address and nothing seems to be missing–'

'Well, I can't really be sure of that, Officer,' I interrupt the man again. His brows snap together, telling me he doesn't like my disruptions. I couldn't care less right now. 'You have to understand,

I helped my daughter move in, but I haven't really been back to her house since then. I wouldn't know if a bag had been taken, if clothes and toiletries were missing, and all that kind of stuff.'

'That's exactly my point, Abi. If that stuff has been taken, then your daughter has gone somewhere of her own free will and sadly just hasn't told you about it. If–' He raises his hand to stop my verbal diarrhoea interjecting again. 'If nothing has been taken, then I'm afraid that still doesn't imply that your daughter is actually *missing*. She no longer lives at home, Abi. She's a grown woman, as hard as that can be for some parents to accept.'

I hear his words – more of the same to shut me up – but I suddenly remember Rose's ruby jewel and reach into my pocket to show Officer Bellamy. Of course, he's quick to tell me there's no way I can know for sure that it's my daughter's, so I tell him all about its history and my aunt and how Rose came to own it. I catch something in his eye. There's something off about this giant of a man, like he's mirroring my own pain in the way he leans closer to me, in the knowledge of his words. Something.

'You're a parent, aren't you?' I ask.

He smiles. It's genuine this time, and actually makes his large chin wobble a little, and his whole face lights up. Officer Bellamy looks like a good man, I decide.

'Yes, I have two daughters. They both studied at the University of Brighton actually, so I'm lucky they were still at home during that time and I could keep some kind of an eye on them. But I can tell you, they pushed the boundaries during their university years. Not just staying out late, but staying out for days. University seems to come with… I don't know, this pass that allows you to run free, never mind the responsible and thoughtful person you were before you started.' He pauses, and I think we both understand he went a little too far with his story. The smile remains, just slightly, and he sighs. 'Anyway, my point is that this isn't uncommon – for parents to feel their child is missing because they haven't heard from them for a little while.'

Officer Bellamy sounds like Adele and Dave, making me feel silly for allowing my thoughts to haunt me these past few days. If I told him about the Patrick situation, would it change his mind? I mean, I can't be sure if Rose – or Dylan for that matter – even know the truth. If they don't, there's no need for them to find out. Despite his own words, Officer Bellamy does probe a little further: what is Rose studying, what's her address, who are her friends? Those kinds of questions. He even asks a little about me being a paramedic. Probably to calm me. And it works… a little. I somehow feel lighter.

Office Bellamy's eyes dance over me for a while. He must be contemplating me and my story, and wondering if it's just that: a story. Something makes him throw me a lifeline.

'I'll pass this on to one of the detectives in the station,' he says, and raises his hand again – a dampener to my own rising hopes. 'I'll explain that I've spoken to you about the piece of jewellery and the fact that this is very unlike Rose. That's all I can do. There are no promises or guarantees, Abi. You have to understand that.'

'Yes, yes, of course. I understand. Thank you so, so much.' I almost choke on my own words. 'What can I do?'

'Well, I should say just go home and wait – and that is what I advise you to do, Abi – because running around Brighton like a headless chicken isn't going to help you or your daughter. She'll come home when she's ready and for all you know she's returned to your London home by now. But I have a feeling you're not the kind of person to listen to that advice.' He pauses and half grins. 'English Literature is studied up on the Falmer campus. You could check it out,' he suggests. 'If you really need peace of mind, some of the students or lecturers may be able to tell you something that might help.'

'You think it's pointless, don't you?' I retort, and don't mean to sound so aggressive after his offer of help.

He exhales deeply, again. 'Yes, I think it's pointless. Brighton is no big city like London, but it's still swarming with people. The parades we have here, and the amount of hen and stag dos that descend on the beach every weekend, would blow your mind.'

I feel my frown deepen. As chirpy as his words are, my previous lightness is being dragged back down with the weight of an anchor. What's he saying, that Rose can never be found because Brighton is such a busy place?

Officer Bellamy lightly chuckles. 'Gosh, I'm sorry, it looks like I've spooked you a bit. I just meant that you're better off going home and waiting to hear from your daughter. It's been a few days – a weekend at that – and, like I said, these students learn how to party and stay out and socialise like you wouldn't believe. Trust me.'

I can't help shaking my head. 'There's no need to trust you, Officer. Like *I* said, as a paramedic in London, I've seen it all.'

The smile that lights his eyes up returns. 'Listen, give me a recent photo of Rose, and your contact number, and I'll request that someone looks into this.'

'I can't thank you enough for taking me seriously. It seems like no one else has.'

The kind man shrugs. 'If I can't even help out a fellow emergency service officer and, well… let's just say I have my own reasons too. I would never forgive myself. Don't expect miracles. Remember I said–'

'I know, I know. Wild students. Happens all the time. I get it, but really, thank you.'

The words fall out of my mouth and I use all my strength not to jump up and hug the man, the first person who has actually promised to help me. My purse only contains a baby photograph of Rose, but we sort a way of me sending Officer Bellamy a picture from my phone – which thankfully hasn't died yet – to his and he jots down all the details he needs. As I'm leaving, something occurs to me and I turn to face him at the door.

'By any chance would you know if Paramedic Science is studied near the Falmer campus?'

'My daughter studied it,' he replies with a smile. 'I guess it's the real reason I decided to help you.'

That's when I realise it was a combination of things that allowed me to thaw this man's heart – I was right when I first met him, he is a kind soul. It was his mercy, not just the emergency services. Paramedic's daughter, police officer's daughter, doctor's daughter, chef's daughter. It doesn't matter what uniform we wear or what we do in our professional lives, what really connects us is our children, and speaking as one parent to another. This stranger is helping me, like I've helped so many others, because he can imagine what it's like to be me right now, to walk in my shoes of fear and not knowing. Where is my child? A simple question, but what a terrifying one if you don't have the answer.

'Anyway,' Officer Bellamy continues, 'that's how I know English and Paramedic Science are both studied over there.'

Wait. *Over there?* Over where? What does he mean? 'How far a walk is it to the campus?'

'Oh no, you wouldn't want to walk it, not from here. It's half an hour on the bus. I doubt you'd find much life up there at this time anyway.'

He peers down at his watch and I take the opportunity to run from the building. I need fresh air. I've caught another lie of Patrick's. Why does Rose live so far from her campus? I thought the whole reason this house was so attractive was because it was close to university. Okay, half an hour on a bus isn't the longest journey in the world, but I'm sure she made it sound like it was a quick walk to her lectures. Hadn't she?

I feel like I can't trust anything: what I know about Rose and her friends and university, everything Patrick has told me, or even my own memories.

Do I really know so little about my daughter? About my daughter's life and what she does? She seems to have a whole life in Brighton that I'm not privy too. When did that happen? I thought we were so close, just the two of us against the world. When did that all change?

The myriad of questions spin in my head. There's a dullness to the street as I walk along the road and to the square. It's not as busy and bustling as it was, and I wonder how long I was in the police station. I didn't give Officer Bellamy a chance to tell me what time of night it is exactly. I peek at my own watch and realise it's gone eight thirty.

Jesus, how did that happen?

The officer's advice of *go home and wait* echoes in my ears over and over again. My mind flashes an image of Patrick in the pub, and it morphs into Rose ambling around the dark and deserted Brighton Falmer campus.

I won't be able to find either of them, will I? He's probably at home with Sadie, having a lovely meal with a glass of wine by the fire, happy in the knowledge that he made sure Sheetal would tell me nothing. And if Rose hasn't even been in her home, why would she be on a campus that is surely closed at this time of night? Why am I aimlessly and helplessly walking around? Everyone I've spoken to has told me that my reaction, what I'm doing, is all a mother overreacting. A mother who has been pushed away from her daughter. But they don't know the whole truth, not like I do. Rose doesn't even know the truth. I hope.

There's probably some fact in what they've all been saying, isn't there? On Friday, Rose called me and possibly didn't even know about the terrorist attack in London because she was busy doing her own thing. Maybe she was even calling me to tell me what that thing was. I haven't heard from her since then because she's busy doing just that, *her own thing*. No, that can't be right... she would have seen the breaking news online surely; even if she hadn't been near a TV, she's always on social media and those sites keep you more updated than the news does anyway.

I am so confused.

Actually, what I really am is a lonely woman who only has her daughter and her job to fill every waking hour. In the hope of not losing one of those things, I've grabbed and squeezed it too tight. Now, Rose is running around lapping up the freedom like she's finally escaped some kind of prison. A prison I created.

I shake my head, wanting to believe all that is true. I feel the ruby gem in my pocket, and can't help but think of Patrick and Dylan Malone. The last of my energy is zapped away as the cold night air whips against my cheeks, as if nature has turned against me too and it's giving me a hard slap in the face. Not to wake me from my confused thoughts, but to punish me for being so helpless.

My feet take me to the train station.

My brain buys a ticket for London.

My body crashes onto my bed.

I give up.

Chapter twenty-four

Dave presses the doorbell and dances from one foot to the other; it's nothing to do with the chilly weather and everything to do with his nerves. If he could, he would wipe his ever-increasing sweaty palms along his dark-blue jeans, but the offerings he's brought from Costa are taking up both hands and halting that.

The nervous feeling is distracting, and he can't fully understand why it seems to have taken over his body, especially his throat. He's worried that he won't be able to utter a word when Abi finally opens the door. If she opens it at all, that is. Dave quickly wonders if his actions are completely unprofessional and he should slowly back away from the door, over the driveway and down the road as fast as possible.

The decision is made for him when he sees her silhouette grow bigger and darker through the glass panels as she approaches the front door. He stops hopping from side to side, stands tall and paints a huge smile on his face – one that he hopes resembles a friendly gesture rather than the look of an obsessive stalker.

As his mind continues to argue with itself about his intentions and friendliness and unprofessionalism, the front door swings back and he's shocked at the state of Abi. The beautiful Abi, who is usually so fresh-faced and impeccably dressed, whose hair is always tidy and clean and whose brown eyes shine when she smiles, seems to have gone AWOL. He's presented with an Abi wrapped in a dressing gown, with her dark hair falling around her face – a woman who looks like she's overslept and hasn't slept in days all at once. Dishevelled is the only way he can describe her, and it leaves him speechless.

'Dave. What are you doing here?' Abi breaks the silence as she rubs the thick fabric of her gown over her eyes like a small child.

I've woken her, Dave concludes to himself. *She looks so… un-Abi-like.*

'I… err, well… Are you okay?' He stutters and frowns, head tilted to one side in complete confusion, and for a second Dave worries that Abi's mother took a turn for the worst. 'Oh my God, Abi, I'm sorry. It's your mum, isn't it?'

It's Abi's turn to scowl, and though she looks bewildered already, there's something in her eyes that doesn't register what Dave's suggesting. Abi's mother must have been a ruse to get out of work. Another un-Abi-like thing.

'You said you needed time off to see your mother…' he prompts, and leaves the information hanging in the air.

Abi's obviously flustered, humming and hawing over what he's said. She attempts to pull back some control. Her eyes open a little wider. She yanks the hair from her face and wraps the strands into a bun using a hairband from her wrist. It's those telltale signs of tripping over her own words and her fidgety body that convinces Dave he's caught her in a lie.

'You didn't take time off to see your mum, did you, Abi?'

She focuses on the ground and shakes her head like a schoolgirl in the headmaster's office. When she returns his gaze, Dave spies the swell of tears puddling in her beautiful eyes and his heartbeat quickens. He hates the hold she has over him and, despite knowing she's lied to get out of work, he steps forward into her home and tells her everything is okay.

* * *

Once the pair are sitting at the dining table in Abi's kitchen, Dave puts down the takeaway coffees and chocolate twists that he brought with him.

'I know they're your favourites,' he says with a gentle smile. 'And to be honest, you look like you need them.'

Something resembling a laugh escapes Abi's pink lips, and she sighs as she wipes the dripping tears away. It's a nice gesture, Dave concludes, like she's thanking him for being honest about how bad her appearance is; she laughs because she understands and agrees but sighs because she's not really laughing at all.

'Want to talk about what's really going on?' he offers. Abi only returns a shrug. 'Is this still about Rose?'

She sips the hot liquid from the red cup and winces. 'Yes, but I really don't have the strength to talk about it, Dave.'

He takes a bite of the pastry and nods his head, content that Abi didn't really lie to him at all about needing time off. She only lied about the person who needed her help. He wonders if maybe he was too unsympathetic about Abi's worries over her daughter. Not wanting to make that mistake again, he keeps quiet and allows Abi to continue with whatever it is she wants to talk about.

'I shouldn't have lied to you about why I couldn't work my shift,' she says, 'and I'm sorry.'

Dave grins and then quickly dusts away the flakes of pastry he feels lingering on his lips and chin. He shrugs his shoulders, hoping it comes across in a cool 'no worries' way. 'Ah, it's fine. Laura and I are getting used to covering for you guys.'

Abi's perfect eyebrows knit together. 'What do you mean? Where's Adele?'

'Oh, you haven't spoken to her?' Dave pauses to swig a mouthful of coffee. 'She called in sick the same evening you said you couldn't work your shift. She hasn't been working either. Doesn't look like she'll be fit to for the rest of the week.' The now raised eyebrows and turned-down lips on Abi's face show she's just as surprised about Adele's illness as Dave had been when he took the call. 'I know, right? I thought the same: Adele the Wonder Woman never gets sick. I think the trauma of Friday finally caught up with her, to be honest. There's only so much we can see as paramedics before it really starts affecting our health. Sometimes it can be physical and sometimes it's mental. Yes, it's the most fulfilling job I've ever done, but I don't think anyone should ignore what a difficult and draining task it can also be to be a paramedic.'

Abi nods and mumbles something about making sure she gives Adele a call. Dave can't help noticing she hasn't touched the coffee, or even attempted the chocolate twist, and his heart aches a small bit. Without thinking, he reaches his hand across the table and lightly holds her fingers. Shock crosses Abi's face, but he's pleased when she doesn't move her hand away from his.

'I can't really stay, Abi. I've got that shift I need to cover,' he says with a wink. 'I hate to leave you like... looking like...'

'I'll be fine.'

'And I don't doubt that for a second. But at the moment you're not fine, and for whatever reason you don't want to talk to me, and that's cool too. I want you to know I'm here for you though.'

A spark of the usual Abi returns when she smiles – it's genuine – and she glows a little bit. 'Thank you.'

'Take the rest of the week. I'll write it up as some kind of compassionate leave or that you're needing a mental break from work after what happened last Friday. Take these next few days and see how you feel. Just don't lie to me, because I want to help, and make sure you let me know how you're doing. Can you?'

As she stands up from the table, letting her hand slide out from under Dave's fingers, she nods and promises to keep him updated. He understands it's an invitation for him to leave as she walks towards the door, and he wonders if that's because he said he needed to leave, or because she actually doesn't want him here any longer.

Back at the front door, he stops to look at Abi. There's no malice there. She's not kicking him out, he decides; she just looks like the saddest woman he's ever laid eyes on.

'Abi, I don't know what's going on, but I want you to know you're a very special woman.'

She turns away from him and grunts air from her nose like a dragon. 'I'm far from that, Dave. I'm an evil woman, you mean. A useless mother whose own daughter doesn't even want to know her.'

So this is all about Rose, Dave thinks, and can't help himself from reaching out and touching Abi's face. He uses his index finger to gently move her chin so she's looking back at him.

'Abi, you have saved so many people.' Dave pauses to graze his finger over her lips to stop her talking. 'Yes, it's your job to do so. It's a job you chose because of who you are. A kind and caring and passionate force of nature who inspires me every time I see you in action. So something has happened between you and Rose – fix it. If that's what it takes to make you feel and look normal again' – they both smile, and he lowers his finger from her mouth – 'then just do it. Just fix it.'

She bites her lip, the front tooth trembling, and picks at the pink flesh for a few moments, and he just watches her, knowing that she's contemplating his words.

'What if I don't know how to just fix it?' she asks.

Dave sighs and gives her a lopsided grin. He wants to have all the answers for her – he wants, more than anything to be able to help her – but these mother–daughter relationships are completely out of his comfort zone.

Then, in one of those foolish cartoon light-bulb moments, he has an answer: 'Go and visit your mum.'

Abi flinches. 'What?'

'I'm not having a go because you fibbed, Abi.' Dave chuckles lightly. 'I mean, surely you and your mum have had your own troubles over the years, so I figure if anyone knows how to fix things with their daughter, your mum must, right?'

She smiles and nods. 'Yeah, I guess.'

'Look, I don't get the whole crazy dynamics of a mother and daughter bond. I do know that mums can give some amazing advice and help.'

Dave knows that's all Abi needed. The beaming smile on her face is testament to that, and it's his time to leave. Something holds him back. He so desperately wants to touch her lips again, this time with his own, but knows that he shouldn't. He *can't*, rather, so he bids Abi one more farewell and walks away.

Chapter twenty-five

As much as I hated seeing Dave on my doorstep, he had a point, and came at precisely the right time. It's funny how things can work out like that; just when you think you're ready to hit rock bottom, you're sent a sign to remind yourself you're not alone. I don't know who sends these signs, and I bet a lot of people think that's a load of rubbish – signs and fate, coincidences or destiny – but I think it's something I believe in. I'd like to think there's someone up there watching over me. Anyway, for me, it's hard not to believe, because at the exact moment Dave had rung the doorbell, I was sitting in my bathroom with my back against the door and a razor blade in my hand. It's something I haven't done for many, many years.

It's difficult to explain, especially to someone like you who is just glimpsing at a moment in my life, and actually, coming from a paramedic, you probably find it far-fetched. I mean, I'm a strong public figure who saves people. But we all have our own demons to fight, regardless of the daily job we do. Let me try and explain, or at least scratch the surface of an explanation.

The first time I self-harmed, it wasn't because I wanted to end my life. Quite the opposite, really; it's because I wanted to *feel* my life. I had seen Patrick with Sadie, *his wife*, for the first time after beginning a relationship with him. The two of them looked so happy and in love, and I guess I knew right then and there that he would never leave her for me. I just chose not to listen to myself. Despite being a student, the lure of drowning myself in alcohol didn't appeal – perhaps due to my studies. Actually, maybe my studies, and the people I had encountered during my training, made the idea of cutting myself something I needed to try.

The first cut was just one slice with the razor along my inner thigh, so it wouldn't be too obvious to anyone. I didn't want someone on my course noticing what I'd done. It hurt, the slice against my white flesh, but it was a different type of pain to what I had been feeling over Patrick and Sadie. It was a pain I could control. It was a release that actually helped me breathe. It was like surfacing from the ocean and inhaling the largest, most satisfying breath. I knew it was wrong. I knew I didn't want anyone to find out what I'd done. It had just been for me, and I promised myself it would never happen again.

It did happen again. The night I discovered I was pregnant. The same night Patrick *officially* dumped me for Sadie. As soon as I saw that first ooze of dark red blood leaking from my thigh again, I hated myself. It wasn't the rush of release and freedom that I had experienced the first time; rather it was shame and guilt and remorse, because it wasn't just my body any longer. Rose was growing inside of me. From that moment on, whenever I felt low or felt I could be spiralling towards rock bottom, I reminded myself that I wasn't so far in the darkest abyss that my daughter couldn't save me, that my child couldn't pull me back to be strong for her. And she always did.

I think it's helped me in my job. There are so many people out there, crying out for help – not attention, real help. Sometimes, I've been the paramedic called to them, and just offering a listening ear and sympathetic tone can do wonders. With others, a little more guidance is needed, and thankfully there are charities who can help people who suffer – charities whose information leaflets I always keep in the ambulance.

Adele once said to me that they make us wear our green uniforms not only for people to recognise us as those who can help, but also for our own good. She believes that when we take it off, it symbolises us being able to let go of all the sad tragedies we've had to witness and deal with on any given shift. I loved my crew member even more after that conversation. I loved knowing that's how she looks at life. I didn't – and still don't – agree, but it's comforting to know there are people like her in this world. Me, on the other hand, I don't shed what I see after my shifts because I don't want to forget the pain. The pain I felt in my twenties, and the pain I witness every day from strangers, is what keeps me going. It's what gets me out of bed, makes me put on that uniform, and it allows me to help those who need me.

Sitting on my bathroom floor, ready to do something I promised I'd never do again... I won't lie, it came as a shock. I didn't realise my mind had returned to the darkness – and the fact that I didn't see it coming was almost as terrifying as actually being there. Could being on my own – no Rose and no job – really be enough to push me over the edge of the canyon and into self-harming again? Or is it the ghosts of the past doing that? I don't know where my daughter is, and everyone's telling me that's fine. It's not, is it?

If you hadn't spoken to your child in over four days, would you worry? Would you listen to friends, and even the police, downplaying the whole thing? Would you let them make you believe that everything is fine and *normal*, because she's a student? Christ, what kind of an answer is that to a parent who can't find their child? I bet if Rose was a smaller child, just ten or even thirteen, and had been walking home from school, every fucker I know would be out in force to search the area. Because she's a grown woman, am I just expected to ignore the fact that I can't find her?

Seriously, what would you do?

Would you slide down your bathroom door, sit on the cold tiled floor and give up?

I did.

Until Dave knocked on my door, that is.

Chapter twenty-six

I've lost all sense of what day it is, and what time it is. Everything seems to have merged into one recently. It's dark when I pull into the hospice car park, that much I know. The temperature has taken a dive and I can't help hoping that Rose is warm, wherever she is. Warm and snuggly – wearing those big fluffy socks she likes – enjoying a hot chocolate and maybe even reading a good book. It's a fantasy, I know, because why wouldn't she be doing that at home if everything were so happy and harmonious? But it's these thoughts that made me put clothes on this evening. It's these images that prodded me to take Dave's advice and come to visit my mother.

There's a comforting warmth in my mother's room. Mum appears to be quite distant as I shed my coat and scarf and pull the chair around the side of the bed so I'm looking at her while I speak. I hate the positioning of the chairs in hospices and hospitals – they always make me feel like I'm so far away from the person I want to be closest to at the time. I pull it closer, practically tucking my knees under my mother's bed, and hold her hand. The action seems to rouse her, and she turns her head to face me.

I don't wait. The door to her room is closed, and it's just the two of us, so I take my chance to speak. I let the words spill as if there is no barrier strong enough to hold them back. A 'flapper-trapper' my grandmother would have called me many years ago, in her strong Northern Irish accent. I'm sure she coined the phrase herself, as I've never heard it said outside of our family. It's usually used when you've had a few too many tipples and you let your mouth run away with you, probably just talking idle gossip, but nonetheless talking too much about things you shouldn't.

And so, here I am, with verbal diarrhoea yet again – I'm really not usually like this – like a drunk woman with a burning secret to share, the epitome of what it means to be a flapper-trapper, telling my mother absolutely everything.

When I've finished, my hitched breaths – in and out, in and out, like I've run a marathon – are all that fill the quiet room. I look over my mother's face, unsure of which version of her is with me, and wonder if she's heard anything of what I've said.

She doesn't leave me hanging, and I watch a seriousness cloud her face as her jaw tightens and her eyes pull away from mine. There's a fluttering in my stomach, one that makes me feel sick. The clenched lines that pull in around my mother's mouth are not the product of a pout, but of anger. The feeling literally oozes out of her face, just in case I was in danger of missing it.

'You're a great mum, Abi, and everything you did was for Rose. I know you truly believe that in your heart,' she says quietly, and a deep line appears between her brows. 'And while I'm a firm believer in not letting your past define who you are, I'm afraid that you have no choice.'

I don't want to speak, but she's glaring at me for a reply. Why is she making this about me and not Rose? I take a large swallow of saliva, giving myself a few minutes, hoping to wet my throat enough that my words won't get stuck there.

'What do you mean, Mum?'

'Stop bloody blaming Patrick Malone for this mess.'

The rise in her decibel tells me I was right to not want to speak, and I don't dare cut in to defend myself. It's my turn to keep quiet and listen, all the while praying she isn't about to drag me to the conclusion that I've tried so desperately to ignore for the past day or two.

'Yes, he's not a nice guy,' she continues, and a tiny bit of spittle flies from her mouth. 'I mean, sleeping with young women, cheating on his wife and betraying his son – he's filthy. I could have told you that over twenty years ago. But my point here is, he didn't start all this. You did. This godawful wretched mess that you and Rose find yourselves in – and those poor bloody men too, actually – is because of you. Own up to the mistake you made all those years ago, Abi, for crying out loud.'

'But… but…'

'But but nothing,' she snaps. She is right too, of course. I can't look at her while she delivers the last dagger. 'While we're talking of being honest, what you did wasn't actually a mistake, it was a choice. You took the easy way out and you lied. Well, I've always said the truth catches up with everyone. Except this time, it hasn't just caught up with you, has it? It's caught up with your precious daughter in a nasty and disgusting web of sex and lies with her biological father and half-brother.'

I throw my head up, not wanting to see my mother's contorted face or squinting and accusing eyes, but her words, and the ugly rawness of them – were just too strong to ignore.

When I say nothing – and really, what in the fuck am I meant to say to my mother's last statement? – she continues her attack: 'Jesus Christ, Abi, own up to what you've done. You're my daughter, my flesh and blood, and I love you. But you haven't been protecting Patrick, you've been protecting yourself. You haven't been thinking about Rose, you've been thinking about yourself. *What will others think of me? What will everyone say when they know the truth? Will I be branded a liar forever?* She's right, those are the questions I've asked myself. It's her tone that I don't appreciate; she sounds like a child in a school playground whinging and moaning. That must be what she thinks of me. 'That's all you're worried about, Abigail. Admit it. Admit that it was your lie that created this revolting predicament. Gosh, that word doesn't even do it justice. It's a mess, Abi, a terrible and sickening mess.'

As if her outburst has completely wiped her out, my mum – the Kitty filled with passion and rage about my life choices – is gone in a heartbeat. The colour in her eyes dims ever so slightly and she looks away, her face expressionless – as if she hadn't just powered through hundreds of words in a matter of minutes. It drained her and took her away from me again. I can't deny a single word she has said. Although part of my brain is telling me to run, escape into the fresh air and gulp it down my burning hot body, I ignore its plea. I won't run away because I don't like what was said. I mean, hell, look at all the energy my mother just used, all the energy that took my mother away. The energy I forced her to use. No, I won't run, I will stay, and I will sit with her, holding her frail and bony hand until she comes back to me.

* * *

It transpires that things aren't exactly that simple when it comes to Mum and her condition. After an hour of sitting with my vacant mother in complete silence, I'm asked – politely – by the nurse on shift to take a break from visiting because Mum probably needs a nap. I wonder then if they heard the raised voices – actually, the raised *voice* because I'd hardly said a word – and the temper coming from my mother. If they did, they don't mention it. I bet they've heard and seen all sorts in here. If it's the place you'll spend your last days before passing over, then it's your right to get things off your chest, I guess. And my mother did just that.

The silence after Mum… went away – for want of a better explanation – wasn't a bad thing. It actually gave me a chance to think. A chance to really absorb the words my mother delivered in her priest-like sermon. Shun yourself from evil, confess your wrongdoings and ask for forgiveness. Could it really be that easy?

No, I don't suppose it could be.

If I admit the lie that I told Rose all those years ago, it won't magically make my daughter appear in front of me or ring my phone. I won't suddenly know where to find her. I'm not daft enough to think it would do any of those things. Maybe, somehow, it would help *me*. Maybe, just maybe, it would mean I'll no longer be stuck in the shadows of my past. Perhaps I could stop secretly feeling like a monster, like a liar, like a failure. Possibly I could even stop overcompensating and throwing my whole life into my job with this burning need to always save other people. It's not those strangers I should be saving at all. Not right now, anyway. I need to start with myself.

As I grip my mother's hand before leaving her alone to recover from her episode, I whisper: 'Rose's life is a mess because of me. Patrick is not the monster. I lied. Twenty years ago, I *chose* to tell my daughter her father was dead, and I never confessed the truth. That one lie has destroyed her life and I'm to blame. No one else.'

Chapter twenty-seven

The cold wind hits me as hard as my mother's words did, but it's amazing the clarity that comes with declaring the truth out loud – even if there's no one around to hear. I said it, finally, and I won't be afraid to say it again. This time, I embrace the cold like I had welcomed the warmth of my mother's hospice room just a few hours ago. A chill makes you feel alive more than the heat can, really. It shakes my body into wanting to do something. The goosebumps rising along my skin remind me that there's life inside me still and, unlike my mother, I can do something – I have the time and the opportunity to put things right.

Her words ring in my ears like the klaxon at the start of a race: '*You haven't been protecting Patrick, you've been protecting yourself. You haven't been thinking about Rose, you've been thinking about yourself.*' My mum has never said a truer thing to me. In that room, the way she spoke to me, the words she used, was done in a way that only a mother can.

I can see that somehow, without me even knowing, I've let this become all about me, and more importantly, I've protected the lie I told. As a parent, how could I do that? This should always have been about Rose. It's not as if I were betraying a friend, or a colleague. This should always have been about my daughter.

I'm obviously running on autopilot because half an hour after leaving the hospice I've driven home and am sitting on Rose's bed in her childhood room. In our house – the place we built our family of two. It's not easy being a single parent, and I won't be the first person to admit that, but does that give anyone the right to play with other people's lives? Does it give anyone the right to determine what they know about where they came from and who they really are? It's what I've done to Rose, isn't it?

The room hasn't changed in the year since Rose left for university. I come in and dust and polish, hoover and, sometimes, change the bedding – Rose has come back to stay on occasion. Other than that, it looks exactly the same as when she lived here. Anyone coming in for the first time would describe it as a girlie room, I think, with its different hues of pink – from the wall paint to the curtains and carpets, from the blankets to the cushions. They all complement each other and give an air of tranquillity and calmness to the room. It's contrasted by Rose's love of all things animal print, with splashes on the rug, the duvet, the artwork on the walls and her various accessories, like her make-up mirror.

The bedroom just screams Rose. Perhaps I've never changed it not because I couldn't, or because she asked me not to, but because I haven't *wanted* to. Sitting here, I can see that the room is my daughter's nature, with its calm and peaceful undertones, which have always been evident in her personality. She's grown from a caring and loving girl into a kind and considerate woman. I made her feel guilty to ask any questions about her father; it would crush her to hurt me or to see me cry, so she never pushed me, unlike so many other people would, I'm sure. Those who would be desperate to know more about the other half of the couple who created them, and therefore would go out of their way to know something, anything, about their biological father. Even back then, I made it about me, and so my beautiful daughter never antagonised me or showed any interest in the subject. Then there's the hint of wildness in the room. I wonder if those bits represent the real Rose, the one who has been hiding from me, the one who does actually want to know who she is and where she came from. Perhaps her wildness is her way of ignoring the fact that she's never had a father and her way of feeling free: move to university, get with a guy, sleep with his father at the same time…

My stomach whirls at the thought.

I breathe in deeply. This time I don't shake the sickening image from my mind. I don't push it away or convince myself that Patrick is a monster who brought this upon us.

It's me. I did this.

I gaze around the room; the dim bedside lamp is the only source of light protecting me from the night shadows trying their best to creep in through the windows. To creep back into my mind. It's impossible to ignore the few that have actually managed to get in. The sway of the long twigs and branches dance on the wall opposite me, tempting me back to the darkness. Back to the place where I wasn't the monster; back to the place where I wasn't the sole reason for the ruining of Rose's life.

As tempting as it is to return, that place no longer exists for me, and I avert my eyes from the prancing silhouettes.

The tears come. I can't stop the gush of emotion from pouring down my face.

As a university student, it was me who nearly broke up a long and happy marriage, and it was me who pushed a woman so far into devastation that she was willing to take her own life. That's what I've truly been defending: myself.

For twenty years I've shielded myself because I believed that leaving Rose fatherless and telling her that he had died so I would never have to face what I did was protecting her. That's a load of bullshit, isn't it? Who am I to make that decision for another human being – daughter, son, sister, whoever? If Rose had known the truth all along, then she never would have…

I gulp down the bile.

If Rose had known that her father was alive, she would have known his name – and Dylan's name – and even if she had decided not to go looking for him, she would have known who he was – who they were – when she met them at the university in Brighton.

What a twisted fate to have met them there, when all along I thought Patrick Malone was tucked away in some dark corner of Scotland, living his own life.

'The truth will always out, for the truth catches up with everyone,' as my mother so simply put it.

If Rose has already found out the truth, there's no telling where she is or what she might have done to herself.

If Dylan knows, there's no denying he will feel just as ruined as she does. If neither of them knows, then the pain of watching them discover what they've been caught up in – thanks to my lie – is a devastating prospect.

It's a lie I can no longer ignore.

Like a right-hook to the side of my head, I know exactly what it is that I need to do.

Chapter twenty-eight

Do you think an only child is a lonely child? Or a spoilt or even selfish child? The former is definitely said quite often, and I suppose it's because, the majority of the time anyway, an only child receives everything, and I'm speaking about things greater than presents and treats. That one child, be it for medical reasons or plain preference, is submerged in the parents' love and time and energy. That one child is front and centre their entire life. Of course, with all that emotion comes the added benefit of the gifts and treats.

I guess that's why people assume an only child is a spoilt child.

It never felt that way when I was growing up. From a young age I was well aware that my mother couldn't have any more children. My parents tried to conceive for years to have me and, just when they had given up being blessed with a baby, my mother fell pregnant. It's always the way, isn't it? When you stop putting pressure on yourself, the thing you want happens, or the idea comes to you, or you find what it is you've been so desperately looking for.

Sometimes, mainly throughout my teenage years, I watched how my friends interacted with their siblings: the fights and arguments, the shared joke or trick, the way they would protect and rely on each other. I'd be lying if I said I never wondered how it felt to live a life with a brother or sister. But I always had my parents, and if I was enough for them, then surely they were enough for me.

Was I spoilt?

Yes, I had pretty much everything I asked for, and my parents gave me their undivided attention all the time, but I've grown into a woman who saves strangers for a living. I don't put myself first.

I want to help others. Surely that proves I wasn't so pampered as a child that I'm a ruined adult because of it.

I can't help thinking that that's the picture I'm painting because… well, would you want to admit to being a spoilt-rotten child?

I won't pretend to remember – it's actually funny how much of our own lives that we forget – but I imagine the loneliness, or rather the being alone, can become quite a dark place. As loved as you are, and despite the attention you receive, you're missing out on that connection. You're missing out on a special bond that only comes with having a brother or sister – or so I imagine – which so many other people have. Does it have a lasting effect on future relationships? Does it make you a stronger person or does it screw you right up?

I'm not even sure why I'm questioning it. Perhaps, after hearing my mother speak to me the way she did, it's got me wondering: if I'd had a sister, would she have put me right all those years ago, in a way only a sibling can? If so, would that mean I would have told Rose the truth many, many years ago? Maybe I wouldn't have lied in the first place. I wouldn't have been allowed to lie. I wouldn't have been allowed to control everything.

Control.

Yes, I'm a paramedic hell-bent on saving others but, deep down, am I so used to getting what I want when I want it, that this profession is another way to stay front and centre? Must I be the hero to get the attention I'm used to? Did I lie to Rose about her father because I wanted to be in control, because I wanted to decide who she would become?

After Rose, the thought of having another child never interested me. I always thought it was because of how I became pregnant in the first place – the secrets and affair behind it, not the deed itself, you understand. Now I can't be sure. If being an only child really has made me attention-hungry and controlling, have I in turn inadvertently passed those qualities – or flaws – on to my daughter?

What have I done to Rose?

Do I really know my daughter at all? Is she a selfish woman, dead set on getting whatever she wants whatever the cost? The past week has proved that I barely know her at all. Despite her not having all the information, she's still a person who is happy to have an affair with her boyfriend's father; she lives miles from the university, when she had made me believe the distance was merely minutes. I don't know any of her friends or where she hangs out, or even what her bedroom looked like before I forced entry into it.

As my mind throws up more and more doubts about Rose, I can't help wondering if this all stems from me. My daughter is my best friend, and we have the closest relationship, but if I'm starting to feel like I don't know who Rose is, could it be because I don't really know myself? I've lied and cheated and had an affair. What else am I capable of?

Chapter twenty-nine

It's windy and drizzling – that fine rain, the type that makes you squint and wets your face in seconds. I'm in Brighton again. I never should have left really, but if I hadn't, my mother wouldn't have been able to put me in my place. Dave wouldn't have been able to remind me that there are beautiful people in the world; people who are kind and considerate for no other reason than just to be that way.

Wait. What? Why am I thinking about Dave? I shake him from my mind and concentrate.

I can't believe I'm walking this same path again. It feels like *Groundhog Day* – if the film were filled with lies and betrayal and sordid secrets. Another image I try to push from my mind, yet it leaves behind a sickening taste in my mouth that will probably never leave.

Patrick and Rose.

It's time to be honest. It's time to confess my lie. It's the only way to uncover what's really happened to my daughter.

I hover at the crossroads of the town. One road leads to the police station and the other to the pub where Patrick took me for a drink. God, that feels like weeks ago rather than days. While I know what I need to do, the way in which I'll go about it is what has made me hesitate. If I turn left, it's to report Patrick Malone to Officer Bellamy, tell the police officer everything from my affair with Patrick to his own with his daughter.

I swallow the fiery sick back down my throat.

Surely, once the police have all the information, they'll realise that Rose isn't merely over-partying with friends, but that Patrick – or Dylan, for that matter – has hurt my daughter in some way.

Or at least that he knows where the hell she is. It's all part of him keeping this secret, something I know only too well: doing whatever needs to be done to keep the control.

If I turn right, it's to plead with the bartender to tell me everything he knows about Patrick and where I might find him. Failing that, I'll hop on a bus over to the university and do everything in my power to obtain Patrick's address. It feels like such a long shot, but there's an urgency deep within me, telling me it can be done – the idea I had before but never had the chance to see it through.

And then a third door opens itself to me and I wonder if it has legs.

Officer Bellamy was a kind man. A parent. A kindred spirit. He's from the area and his daughter studied Paramedic Science at the university. Surely one, if not both of them, have access to Patrick's address. Even if I don't tell him the whole dirty truth of our mixed-up relationships, I'm sure Bellamy will tell me. Won't he? Could he actually give me that information? As lovely as he was yesterday, he did seem quite straight. It's one thing to ask a copper to find your maybe missing daughter; it's quite another to make him give you a university professor's address.

As I take a step in my chosen direction, the decision is yanked away from me. There's the sound of a prolonged car horn. The screech of tyres on the wet ground. The impact of metal crushing bone.

Chapter thirty

My body reacts so quickly, it's as if my brain hasn't needed to communicate with it at all. Just like when I attend any job, the moment I jump from the ambulance, full concentration mode is in play. Adrenaline takes over. This isn't like the high you get from bungee jumping or that first pull on a morning cigarette. A paramedic's adrenaline is a methodical and calming one. It means I can face each job with a stillness that allows me to see past the blood and broken bones and assess each patient's needs. It means I have the confidence to rush into a situation with authority and reassurance and take command of what needs to be done.

Right now is no different.

It all happened at once. As I lifted my foot to turn in the direction of the police station, a person lightly nudged my shoulder, but it happened swiftly, as if they were running past me. It was then the driver, who simultaneously slammed his hand on the horn and his foot on the brake, who caught my attention and caused me to spin around in time to see the woman – the figure who had breezed past me just seconds before – run out into the road. The driver's wheels were no match for the heavy downpour of the last week and, instead of coming to an emergency halt, the car slid at some speed into the woman. Screams and gasps could be heard as the bumper smashed into the slim woman, sending her crashing onto the bonnet before ricocheting down to the wet gravel. A crowd gathered in moments. Through all that turmoil, I couldn't help noticing the bag flying in slow motion from the woman's hand. My eyes focused on a single can of Diet Coke – Rose can drink at least four a day, despite my protests – as it spun

151

through the air, cracked on the ground and sprayed dark, frothy liquid like a Catherine wheel firework.

I don't recognise her at first. I'm too busy going through the motions: the woman is unconscious, with no obvious head wounds, with a broken right femur which has punctured through the skin. Priority is given to limiting the amount of blood loss, and I tear my wet jacket from my body. I use the material to create some kind of gauze in an attempt to put pressure on the gushing blood without disturbing the cracked bone, which is on show for everyone to see. I make a decision, despite being alone, to apply manual traction in an attempt to realign the femur bone. It means pulling the woman's leg straight until the paramedics arrive, but in the long run, it's the best thing for the patient.

'Call an ambulance,' I yell, though I'm sure – as is the way in these circumstances – this task will have already been done. The poor call centre will probably have received numerous calls from a variety of bystanders about the same incident. It happens all the time. Better than no one phoning at all, I say.

The crowd doesn't disperse; people like to watch a crisis unravel like a soap opera until the very end, if possible. I keep talking to the woman. There's always hope that unconscious patients can hear, but my eyes are roaming her entire body, looking for other injuries. I feel lost without my bag. There's only so much I can do without my tools.

Luckily, the wait isn't long, and the surge of two people clad in starched green uniforms taking over from me happens in an instant. As they set to work on the broken woman, I explain who I am and relay what exactly happened, what the patient's visible injuries are, and observations on her breathing. They take it all in without looking at me once – it's what we do. Our hands, eyes and minds are everywhere, but we're calm and controlled.

Control.

It's where I find myself again – in the middle of it, demanding it, seeking it. In control. Despite being caught up in my own disaster, I've somehow allowed myself to be submerged in someone else's catastrophe and demanded the attention and authority.

The male paramedic swoops in with a traction splint and applies it to the woman's leg; I can finally let go of the patient. I wipe my bloodied hands up and down my jeans as I stand up, my kneecaps wet and my thighs stained with a stranger's bodily fluids.

'Hello, love, can you hear me? I'm a paramedic and my name is Fiona,' the petite red-headed woman explains. 'We're going to take you directly to the hospital.'

The male paramedic works quickly and quietly, grabbing the board to transport the woman.

'Does anyone know this woman? Is anyone with her?' The red-headed paramedic speaks to the crowd – without looking at them – as she seamlessly helps her crew member lift the woman from the ground.

When I stand back out of their way, and take in the scene in its entirety, I release a long and staggered breath. I know the patient. I know the woman.

'I'm coming with you,' I whisper.

The male paramedic runs from the van's back door to the front, obviously the driver, and the redhead frowns at me. She clearly thinks there's no need for me to attend. I've done everything I can. The woman is their patient.

I shake my head, wishing that the action would somehow explain what I mean. It doesn't.

'It's... I-It's...' I clear my throat and pull my shoulders back in an attempt to sort myself out.

Jesus. Shit. Fuck.

How did I not realise earlier? What the hell is wrong with me?

'I know her... the patient,' I say while pushing my way into the back of the ambulance. 'Her name is Sadie Malone.'

Chapter thirty-one

It's strange how the last hour has whizzed by me so fast, yet everything also feels like it's in slow motion.

I'm sitting in the corridor of the hospital, just outside the cubicle Sadie was rushed into. Sadie Malone. Wow.

It's hardly surprising that I didn't recognise Patrick's wife at first. It's been a long time. Yet, the moment I realised it was her, how could I have worked on her injuries and not known? She looked just as beautiful as she always did – despite the violent car accident. Flawless skin, with make-up so perfect I never could understand how she applied it in such a way that made her look... well, perfect. Hair still as golden as the sun on a summer's day, just as it always was; not a touch of grey or darkened roots. The petite figure of a woman who you would think attended spinning classes every single goddamn day. I clearly remember Patrick telling me his wife was more interested in strolling around museums and galleries than pounding the running machines or bicycles in a gym.

Sadie is the total opposite of me. In looks and personality.

Who knows what urged me to jump in that ambulance with her? It was an automatic response, and not because I care if she's okay. That sounds awful, I know. You have to remember that this woman has the life I should have had. The only logical reason for coming with the paramedics, and Sadie, is because I knew someone at the hospital would contact Patrick. My body has only just caught up with my mind, so apparently, I do in fact know exactly what urged me to come with them. He's the person I was looking for. I wanted his address. Sadie was sent to me as a sign. This is how I'll find Rose.

I'm not completely heartless. I'm sorry that Sadie had to be hurt, again because of me, but nothing comes before my daughter, my best friend.

Despite enlightening the nursing team that I'm a paramedic from London, they are refusing to let me in to see Sadie. I have to wait for her husband, so I've been told.

The more I think about what I need to do, the less I want Patrick here. The nerves tingling inside my body are making me feel like a teenager on my first day at school, wanting to walk through the classroom door and embrace my future, while at the same time wanting to relinquish all responsibility, run home and enjoy a duvet day. Ha! There're no fucking duvet days in a grown-up world. I need to bite the bullet.

Sadie was never the sign, the beacon to bring Patrick to me. She's the answer to all of this. It's Sadie I need to be honest with; she needs to know about Rose.

A doctor and nurse breeze through the blue curtain of Sadie's cubicle, pulling the starchy material back behind them, discussing the woman's positive progress and reactions. She's not unconscious any more. It's now or never. I feel like Bambi – in that scene when the poor thing is learning to walk on the ice for the first time. Like a fawn who can barely stumble ahead of itself, and my feet – as heavy as blocks of cement – seem unhappy about the move I'm making.

I have to tell Sadie the truth.

'What the hell are you doing here?' His voice is low, the words are said through gritted teeth, and his breath is hot on my skin.

Without thinking, I exhale a large puff of air, almost as if I've been saved by the bell. Am I really not ready to tell the truth?

Patrick grabs my arm; his large fingers protrude into my flesh so tightly that I yelp as he drags me to the fire exit opposite us. None of the staff milling about the ward bat an eyelid.

'They said she was helped by an off-duty paramedic,' he sneers, and releases me with a small shove, but big enough to make me cascade into the grey brick wall of the stairwell. 'Never in my wildest dreams did I think it would be you. What the fuck are you doing back here?'

The venom in his words. The spit that ejects from his mouth. The darkness in his eyes.

I can't pinpoint what it is exactly, but there's something in Patrick that lights the fire within me; only this time, it's not a blaze of passion. It's of hate.

'How dare you?' The veins in my neck contract as my temper blows like an unstable volcano. 'You know exactly why I'm here. I want to know where Rose is, and I want to know now.'

For a minute, Patrick genuinely looks taken aback. 'What's that got to do with me?'

And there he is, the lying Mr Malone I know... and loved. He has no power over me now. I won't let him manipulate me, control me, not again. I march towards him with my finger pointing and say, 'I know your affairs haven't stopped with my daughter, you disgusting piece of shit. I saw you with Rose's housemate.'

'Sheetal,' he replies, a little too quickly, and from the low groan and closed eyes, it's obvious he didn't mean to get caught out so easily.

'Ha! Yes, Sheetal, you flaming idiot. You're either shagging her or blackmailing her.'

'Blackmailing her? Abi, what in God's name are you on about?'

'She knows where Rose is. You've told her not to tell me. She's obeyed your order like all good students do, and that's either because she's infatuated with you or because you've got dirt on her that you've promised to tell all.'

'Abi, listen—'

'I saw you with your son too. Dylan.' I spit out his name, the anger fully taking over my body. I can't see a way of stopping. 'If I'm wrong about Sheetal, then... then it's Dylan. You and he are in cahoots. You've done something to my Rose. You've harmed her and... and... he didn't look very happy when I saw him with you. Come on, I'm right, aren't I? Tell me, Patrick. Tell me I'm right.'

The tears come, slightly unexpectedly. What do I expect when I allow my emotions to take over like that? The air in the corridor is suffocating and I can't help crouching down, my fingertips resting on the floor help me balance, and I inhale as though I'm an asthmatic.

'Jesus Christ, woman, get up,' Patrick says, and pulls me again. The same spot of skin as before. It feels tender. I'll bruise, I'm sure. 'Stop doing this. I don't know what you're playing at, but you need to get out of here,' he continues. I won't budge. 'I need to see Sadie and you need to leave.'

He yells the final word; there's something in his tone of voice. Sadness? Regret? I can't be sure. 'What happened? Please just tell me and I'll go.' I can certainly hear the begging tone in my own voice.

Patrick releases me. The look of a cartoon raging bull returns to his reddened face. 'Fine, look, you're right about Dylan. Not Sheetal.'

'Right about what? Dylan's hurt Rose? What's he done to her? I swear to God, if he's hurt her I'll kil–'

'Fuck's sake, Abi, calm down. This isn't an episode of *Luther*.' Patrick reaches out and places a hand on the door handle; I'm unsure if it's to stop anyone interrupting us or if he's planning to leave and give me no further information. He would happily leave me in limbo again, give no details, no explanations. Finally, he says, 'Dylan discovered there was something going on with me and Rose.'

His lips turn down. He feels as sick as I do.

'You mean he knows? He knows that you and Rose...' I can't.

Patrick sighs. 'I don't exactly know what Dylan knows. He was talking in riddles, angry and confused. I'm sure he was–'

'Does he know? Does he know that Rose is... is your–'

'No, don't be ridiculous.'

'This needs to end now, Patrick.' I notice the beads of sweat forming at the top of his head. 'We all need the truth to be out in the open. As despicable and' – I swallow the bile snaking its way up my throat – 'sickening as it is, we need to clear this mess that we… that I started.'

A man bounces down the stairs and halts anything Patrick was about to say. The silence can actually be felt; it's like acid on the skin, the awkwardness and fear burning deeper and deeper–

'Thanks,' the stranger says as Patrick opens the door for him.

The interruption is annoying and uncomfortable. Wasting time. I can't take much more of this.

'Abi, I need to get inside. I need to see my wife.' He holds up his hand, silencing me. 'Yes, I know you need answers, and I have them. I'll explain everything that Dylan told me. Just not here. Not now. Please.'

'I'm not leaving, Patrick. I don't care. I'm not going anywhere until I know–'

'Okay. Alright.' He interrupts me again, this time with an exasperated sigh. 'Wait for me downstairs. In the car park, the small one at the side of the hospital. Let me just see Sadie and make sure she's alright. She at least needs to know I'm here. The doctors need to know her husband hasn't ignored their call. Okay? Can you do that?'

I shrug. Is there really any argument to be had? Ten minutes ago, I thought I had to tell all to get what I wanted, but finally, Patrick is going to confess to what he or his bloody son has done. I'm about to get what I want: my daughter.

'Okay.'

Patrick's irritation is clear from his flared nostrils and pinched lips. 'Fine,' he replies. 'Give me twenty and I'll meet you downstairs. I'll tell you everything you want to know.'

Chapter thirty-two

Patrick lied; there is no small car park at the side of the hospital. Well, there obviously used to be one here. I can see the faded white paint lines marking the bays and a broken pay and display machine is still standing, just about. It's a disused area, a work in progress. Whatever it is, it's giving me the creeps. When did it get so dark that the lamp posts were needed? This place, this *car park*, is surrounded by a metal fence, with huge trees overshadowing it, and there's barely any light here – just the slither from the lamp posts shining around the corner. Why would Patrick tell me to wait for him here?

He's trying to intimidate me.

That's exactly what he's up to. That bastard thinks he can freak me out like this? Thinks I won't hang around and demand the answers he's promised me? He can't scare me, and he certainly can't get rid of me. I'll give him the precious minutes he begged for with his wife, the perfect Sadie, and that's it. Then I'll–

The pain in my head is excruciating, but it's the utter shock of what's happening that causes my heart to beat so fast I can barely catch my breath.

His fingers are wrapped so tightly around a clump of my hair it feels as if it's about to be pulled from the roots. I've had my hair pulled, but this is different. It burns and stings and my hands automatically reach up and around in an attempt to keep the strands in place. But his fist isn't budging. In fact, it only twists further, increasing the fire inside my skull, as he forces me forward. I'm pushed with such force that my face slams into a brick wall.

Pushed and pulled like a rag doll.

His hands controlling everything I do.

I know it's him. I don't need to ask, and there's no point in calling out for help; Patrick told me to meet him here for a reason. I can't see his face. I can imagine the anger brewing in his eyes – although with the violence he's showing against me, the anger is obviously no longer *brewing*.

After all these years, Patrick still smells like Patrick. I don't mean he's wearing the same aftershave as when I knew him in Scotland, but I mean his smell… him. Do you know what I mean? When you know a person so well, you know everything about them – including their personal scent. It was something that used to warm me, something that used to make me feel safe when I was wrapped in his arms and feeling loved. Now it's a smell that revolts me. It's a smell that makes me heave. It's unstoppable. I retch and vomit down the wall; splatters of it bounce off the brick and land on my coat.

'For fuck's sake, Abi,' he snarls. He must think that I'm scared, that my bodily reaction to him is out of fear. 'I'm not going to hurt you. Well, not now, but this is a warning.'

Patrick doesn't release my hair. He keeps me pinned to the wall, but there's less pressure against my face and the brickwork.

'W-what do you mean?' I whisper. 'A warning?'

'Back the fuck off, Abi,' he whispers too, right in my ear; but his whisper is filled with malice. 'Stay away from me and my wife. And my son, for that matter, or I promise you, you will regret it.'

'Patrick–'

'Come near my family and…' His fingers yank hard on my hair again. 'Jesus Christ, Abi, why did you have to…? Stay away or I'll fucking kill you. I mean it.'

I would laugh at how much Patrick sounds like some macho movie villain if I didn't believe him so much. I can hear the hate in his voice. Why? Surely I should hate him more than he hates me. What doesn't he want me to find out so badly that he would risk this? He must know a member of the hospital staff could see us at any moment. He must know I could go to the police and report his threat. He must…

My thoughts are thrown to another place, a darker place in my mind, and I wonder if his words are so frightening because they feel so real. Would he hurt me? Is Patrick capable of that?

Abruptly, he loosens his grip on me, but his flattened palm remains on the back of my head, silently instructing me not to turn around. The pain in my face, from the smash against the brick wall, intensifies, and I feel the blood trickle down my cheek.

'Abi, I'm leaving. Sadie wants to see her son and I'm going to collect him. You can't still be here when we get back. You have to leave.' Patrick's sigh is deep and ragged. 'I meant what I said. Leave, Abi, for your own sake.'

There's something in Patrick's voice as he pushes my head away from his large hand. It's hard to describe but it *sounds* malicious and nasty and… truthful. I wait until his footsteps are a distant patter on the pavement before I let the tears fall. My chest feels heavy with every laboured breath I take. Have you ever cried so much that the pain in your chest actually hurts, hurts like a sharp knife is stuck in its core? Ever cried so hard that the heavy feeling in your chest feels so real and so intense, you think you'll be crushed by your own sadness?

That's exactly how I feel, because it would appear that Patrick can also be added to my growing list of people I don't really know.

Chapter thirty-three

The tears have stopped running down my cheeks, but their tracks have left a dryness – an everlasting stain on my skin – mingled with the dry blood. After I slithered down the wall like a snivelling coward, I used the sleeve of my jumper to stop the blood trickling from the cut on my head. My arse was cold at first. Now I feel nothing. I'm numb, and not just in the nether regions, but all over my body, internally and externally, physically and mentally. I feel *nothing*.

I've been staring ahead at the trees swaying in the wind for some time. It feels like it's been days; it hasn't, obviously. And I haven't really been paying much attention to the trees at all. I haven't been paying much attention to anything. Since the terrorist attack my mind has been filled, practically bursting, with different thoughts and images: Rose running away; Rose lost or battered and left for dead; Rose and Patrick; my mother yelling at me; Rose and Patrick; Dave extending a kind hand to me (why would he do that?); Adele laughing at me for overreacting; Rose and Patrick; that girl in the saree keeping things from me, hiding the murder weapon for Dylan; Rose and Patrick; my mother being tied to the bed by the orderlies; Rose and Patrick.

I scream, a shrill and piercing screech, as if I'm trying to expel my pain and confusion into the world like a banshee. Shit, that describes me to a tee: a wailing woman in mourning – mourning the loss of her daughter, her mother, the life she could have had, because nothing is as it was. I don't have the same tight-knit relationship I used to have with my daughter, my mother flips between knowing who I am and thinking I'm the hired help, and Sadie is living the blissful married life that I should have had. Then there's the long unkempt hair, the pale skin, the red eyes from all the weeping. I'm a banshee.

No! What am I doing?

I'm feeling sorry for myself. I'm letting my mind go to places that I have neither evidence nor reason. I'm telling myself I'm a mythological Irish creature, for fuck's sake. This isn't about me, this is about Rose – this is about my daughter and her safety, for crying out loud – and I need to pull myself together.

Just like my mother said, I need to stop making this about me. Rose's life has been ruined because of what I've done, and God knows what's happened to her off the back of that lie.

With the image of my mother lying in her care home bed – giving it to me straight – in my head, I pull myself up from the cold hard ground and march towards the hospital entrance. It would be so easy for me to run away, to do as Patrick warned and stay away from his family. I mean, he's only protecting them.

But screw him, because that's exactly what I'm doing too.

I refuse to run away and hide from the truth any more.

I refuse to lie.

With my new-found strength, I storm through the automatic doors and head for A&E, and the cubicle Sadie was in. I don't know what state she'll be in now, or how long it'll be until Patrick returns with his son. I have to at least try and speak to this woman. The heavy blue curtains are still drawn, and I can't make out if there's anyone standing around the bed behind them. I clock the red-headed paramedic standing at the reception station and make a beeline for her.

'Hi, do you remember me?' I ask as she turns around.

Her smile is beautiful, wide and genuine. 'Yes, of course. Thanks for your help with the patient. Quick thinking, covering her wound and applying manual traction, but then you're a fellow paramedic, so what else would you have done?'

I return the smile, giggle slightly and try to engage her in some professional banter. 'Well, we're never really off-duty, are we?'

'No, you could say that.'

'The amount of phone calls and text messages I receive from friends and family asking what they should do about the burn on their arm or the boil on their flaming arse, you'd think I offer a private service,' I say, with an added laugh.

It's all lies, but these are different lies. These are fibs; they won't hurt anyone. Plus, there is some truth to it: Laura from work is forever telling me that she has friends who constantly message her when one of their kids falls over or hurts themselves and they want her opinion. One time, Laura's sister walked into the corner of the bedframe and busted her foot – you know, that blinding pain when you walk into the bed – and she thought she had broken her little toe. Laura gave her step-by-step instructions on how to strap it up, because that's all they would have done at A&E. She saved her sister a trip to the hospital, anyway. I'm hoping this paramedic can relate to Laura.

'Oh my God, ain't that the truth,' she says, with an exaggerated hand-throw in the air. 'Just the other day, my best friend called me because her four-year-old son whacked his head on the coffee table, and she wanted me to go round to her house on the double.'

The redhead continues with the story, and I know I have her. The connection with Laura's experiences is therefore a connection to me, and I have my way in. When she's finally finished recounting her tale, she seems more at ease, more comfortable with me and less professional.

'How's Sadie doing?' I ask. 'The nurse said her husband is on his way, but I'm worried that her being alone will freak her out.'

The redhead frowns in a tell-me-more way. 'Really?'

'Oh yes. Poor Sadie has suffered with panic attacks in the past. I didn't want to step on your toes – you were the attending paramedic after all, and I'm sure you have to get on – but I hate the idea of her being alone. The shock she must be feeling from what happened.'

She bats her hand. 'You're not stepping on my toes. As I'm sure you know, we'd love to hang back and make sure every patient is okay after their traumatic experience, but now we're finished with the handing over and the write-up, it's back to the road for us.' As if on cue, the male paramedic beckons her from his position at the ward's entrance. 'Your friend is in cubicle four. Go and wait with her until the family arrives. Duty calls.'

The redhead says goodbye. It's her description of Sadie that echoes long after she's walked away. *Your friend.* She's hardly that, but I've been given the permission I need and turn in the direction of where Sadie is. This time, I don't hesitate, I don't wait for someone to drag me back. I swallow the lump in my throat and march forward.

Chapter thirty-four

I won't bore you with the details of our *I-said-she-said* chat – you know the story well enough by now – but needless to say, I left Sadie in a worse state than I found her in. She is bruised and battered externally, thanks to the car ploughing her down, but she now has those scars internally too, thanks to me verbally bashing her with abhorrent details that no one would want to hear.

One thing she did say, and which will haunt me forever, was how, because of what I had told her about Rose and Patrick, she wished she died all those years ago in Scotland. She actually wished – and I could tell she meant it by the painful way she closed her eyes and let the silent tears escape – that she had been successful in taking her own life. That blame lies with me.

Do you think she wished that because then there would be a chance that Rose would have known her father? There would have been no reason to lie about his death if she hadn't had been in the picture. Or do you think it's purely because she wouldn't have had to hear those words or picture those vile images in her mind, which I'm sure are scorched on her brain like they are on mine? Her husband slept with his own daughter.

I swallow the scream threatening to explode from within.

Maybe it's me who should have ended my life all those years ago in Scotland. If I had, none of this would have happened. Or perhaps I should have chosen to tell the truth when I was a young mum finding her way in life. Either way, the truth will always out, just like my mum tried to warn me.

As I step out of the hospital, I don't care if I bump into Patrick and his son. There's a glimmer of relief in my chest, allowing me to breathe easier. Surely it can't just be because I've told my secret to someone after all this time?

Yes, of course it is.

I've carried that secret with me for so long, told no one except my mother – who quickly forgot she knew the truth which, as awful as it is to admit this, has always worked in my favour – and it has slowly eaten away at me.

The relief that has come with telling Sadie doesn't outweigh the feelings of regret and dread that still darken me. I do feel somewhat lighter. Just slightly. Just enough to know it was the right thing to do.

The wave of weightlessness flowing through me is short-lived when that inner darkness reminds me that I have no idea what I'm doing. Spinning round, I wonder where in the hell I actually am. The sign on the hospital tells me I'm just leaving the Royal Sussex County Hospital. Not that that makes me any the wiser of where–

I don't hear the ping of an incoming text message, but the vibration inside my pocket disturbs my thoughts, and I pull out my mobile phone. My heartbeat quickens when I see a number that I don't recognise – I wish the phone had been set to preview the first few lines of the messages before opening them. It's as if I need a little teaser of what's to come. It's rare to receive a text message as it is – everyone I communicate with either uses WhatsApp or makes an old-fashioned phone call. To receive a text message from a number that I don't have stored in my phone… that's what's got my heart beating like a drum.

What if it's that officer I spoke to? Maybe a search for Rose has started because of some vital evidence they've found. No, the police wouldn't give me that information via a bloody text message. What if it's Patrick? What if he's watching me with his son from the shadows of those trees? He knows I've spoken to his wife and he's playing with me, taunting me, before he fulfils his warning. No, there's no way he could have my number, is there? Knowing my luck, it'll just be someone from work asking me to cover their shift.

Just open the damn message, Abi – a screech comes from inside my head; the banshee is still in there somewhere.

My fingers shakily dance over the screen, tapping in my passcode because my thumbprint didn't work – must be the sweat. Why am I so nervous about a bloody text message? The rarity of one, like I just concluded to myself – that has to be the reason. I hold my breath as I click on the unknown number and nearly drop the phone. Taking a second to readjust my grip, my fingers locking themselves around the iPhone, I also let the air, which had been holding tight in my lungs, escape. Through teary, blurred eyes I read the message over and over again:

Mum it's Rose, call me.

Chapter thirty-four

Rose is alive. Rose is safe.

Oh God. It's like a mantra singing in my head. Rose is alive and Rose is safe. Rose is alive and Rose is safe. I'm almost skipping down the road.

Did I really think there was a chance Rose might be dead? I stop and think. Yes, if I'm honest with myself, I thought that was the only possible explanation for her not getting in touch with me.

That doesn't matter now; I can't even begin to explain to you the feeling of relief filling my body at this exact minute. Wait, I can. It's as if my chest was shackled inside a metal cage for nearly a week, and every single breath I took was painful and full of fear. I felt guilty for breathing when I had no idea where my child was or what state she was in.

It's okay now. All is right with the world again, because I rang the unknown number that had texted me. It was Penny's, Rose's housemate, and the pair had been away somewhere. I don't have all the details. As soon as Rose told me that she was home – her Brighton home – I explained I wasn't far.

Oh God, it's back. That gnawing pain in my chest.

I remember why I'm close to Rose's house: because I was at the hospital which, luckily, is only a fifteen-minute walk from hers, and because I was with Sadie and Patrick and… I gasp for air, feeling the restrictions of that cage trying to enclose around my chest again. My joyful skip is rendered to a slow walk, and a dark cloud descends over me as I realise that the reunion with my daughter won't be full of hugs or laughter at our miscommunication. It will be one of confessions and tears.

Do I have to tell Rose? By her tone of voice on the phone, it's pretty obvious she doesn't know the truth. She actually sounded excited to speak to me.

I hate myself. How can I even debate whether or not to tell Rose the truth? It's no longer a choice. The truth is already out there, whistling in the wind, preparing to be next week's gossip – because dark lies like this always become Chinese whispers. This is my wrongdoing and I need to be the one who tells Rose. It felt so good confessing to Sadie. Perhaps this will also give me an unburdening feeling – I know, deep down, that Rose has always wanted to ask questions about her father. If I can do this, Rose will understand why I lied in the first place... Yes, I lied to protect myself, but really, it was also about protecting her.

I shake off the feeling of dread. I literally shake my arms loose, away from my body, and stretch my neck from side to side as my legs lead the way; the way that's being shown to me by the little figure on the map on my phone app.

Standing in front of Rose's student house, I'm taking a moment to steady my breathing and hoping my legs will stop trembling when my phone sparks to life in my hand. It's a number I know, a number I know well, and I ignore it. A rush of guilt punches my stomach – I never disregard a call from my mother's care home but, right now, it's about prioritising. The nurse will be calling about my mother having another episode, calling for me and needing me to calm her down. Sadly, as much as she needs her daughter, the need to see my own daughter outweighs her demands.

Everything around me is a blur, hazy and unfocused, until Rose opens the front door. I exhale so deep my body lurches forward, and I drink in every ounce of her appearance: long, straight, shiny hair as black as coal, flawless white skin and bright red lips. Her figure has filled out since she left home for university, but it's healthy and she carries the extra weight fantastically in a close-fitting jumper dress.

'Mum.' Her voice. Her tone. Hearing my name, it's all too much and the tears – happy tears – spring from my eyes uncontrollably. 'Oh my God, Mum, what's wrong? Come inside.'

Rose tucks me under her arm, leads me into the house, further down the corridor and into the living room, and ushers me onto the couch. She offers me a cup of tea, but I can't let go of her hand and I plead with her to sit next to me. I just need to look at her face, hear her voice again, to know that she really is okay.

'I'm so sorry I didn't call you again, Mum,' she explains. 'I had no idea about the terrorist attack in London. Not until I came home today and Sheetal told me you were here... and about what happened in town. It was on your shift, wasn't it?'

I merely nod. It's all I can offer as I wait for the tears to dry up. Rose is babbling on. Her lips are moving quickly, her focus fully on me. I see the worry in her beautiful brown eyes and realise I'm probably scaring her. I clear my throat and don't let go of her hand.

'Everything is fine,' I croak. 'I mean, obviously not in London – the situation was terrible – but that all seems like a distant memory to me now. Where have you been? I've been so worried. I went to the police and–'

'Wait, what?' Rose interrupts. 'Why the hell did you go to the police?'

Her tone has changed. She sounds annoyed, pissed off even. Another one who will think I totally overreacted about the entire thing.

'Well, when you didn't reply to any of my phone calls or messages, when you weren't at home posting on Snapchat, I thought... well, I thought a lot of things, mainly bad things.'

'Bad things?' She echoes my words with a frown and a curl of the lip. 'What the hell are you on about, Mum? I left you a voicemail on Friday.'

'Y-yes, I know...' I stutter and hesitate; *Christ, pull yourself together, Abi.* 'I couldn't really understand what you said in your message. It wasn't very clear, it–'

'Damn this bloody house.' I'm momentarily stunned by her anger. 'The reception in this place is crap. We can barely ever make calls or use the Internet without needing to step outside into the back garden. I made that call from my room upstairs, and that's probably the worst possible place for reception. I'm sorry, Mum.'

It's my turn to frown. 'I don't understand. What did you say in the message? All I really got was that you were sorry and that Dylan knew.' I gulp hard, sure that a bead of sweat runs from my forehead at the mere mention of his name.

Rose breaks my gaze, and my hold of her hand, and starts to fidget. 'I went away with Penny. It was a spur of the moment thing. I hadn't planned to go with her.'

'So why couldn't you reply to any of my missed calls? Why didn't you know about the attack in London?'

She sighs, in a way that makes me feel like she can't be bothered to explain her goings-on to me. When did that become a thing? We always had great chats about our adventures. Well, Rose's adventures. I could only tell her about work stuff.

'Penny had been planning this glamping retreat for weeks, it's all she talked about, and she was due to travel Friday afternoon. Then, Thursday night... well, something happened, and she insisted I go with her. It had a strict no phone policy – no technology, actually – so there were no phones, TVs, radios or computers there. It was about taking time for yourself in this social media-crazed world and, like I said, something had happened, and it was just what I needed.'

And there it is, my window to tell Rose the truth, to tell her I think I know what the *something* is. First, my thoughts mock me, openly laugh at me for thinking she ran away or that she was dead or that Patrick killed her. My job really has had an effect on me. Just like Officer Bellamy said, Rose went on a trip with a girlfriend – okay, not partying away the weekend like he thought, but still, he was right. My mind pauses on the large officer for a moment, when I think about why I didn't tell him about Patrick and his involvement with my daughter. I had a chance to tell the police about Professor Malone: the lying, cheating monster who destroyed my daughter. Why was I protecting him? As I look into Rose's eyes, I know exactly why I didn't tell Officer Bellamy about Patrick in that police station. I wasn't protecting Patrick. I wasn't even protecting Rose – which is what has always got me through this lie. I was protecting myself. I lied to my family to protect myself. Just like my mother said. She was completely right.

'Mum, what's going on? You're so pale.' Rose sparks me back to the here and now. 'I mean, I get that you must have been worried if you didn't understand my voicemail, but this is a bit extreme. Actually, I can't find my phone.' Rose interrupts herself with a new train of thought. 'After I left you that voicemail, I switched off my phone and put it in my bedside table – I knew I would be tempted to check it if I brought it with me and, really, the last thing I needed was to hear from Dylan–'

She stops herself short and I feel the emotions rising in me again, getting stuck in my throat and threatening to choke me. *The phone, Dylan… tell her the truth.*

Tell her the truth, my mind screams at me.

I have no choice. The truth is the only option here. No more lying to my daughter.

'Rose.' My voice is a whisper. 'This something that happened. I know what it was.'

My daughter's face contorts right in front of my eyes – the look of concern *for* me becomes one of fear *because* of me. Her neck tightens as she attempts to swallow her saliva and speak, but what comes out are only stuttered sprays. I think she was trying to ask: *how do you know?*

I hold up my hand to stop her from trying again. There's no need to put her through the agony of asking me questions, dodging my interrogations and trying to come up with a quick lie or story.

'R-Rose, I know about Patrick Malone.' Her jaw drops open, and my heart pounds so rapidly that I have to open my mouth wide to inhale and exhale fast enough. 'But there's something I need to tell you. Something you need to know about Patrick. I've lied to you all your life, Rose. Now it's time you knew the truth.'

Chapter thirty-four

She doesn't scream. She doesn't lash out. She doesn't sob.

Rose sits there, her hands clasped together and wedged between her thighs as if in prayer. Perhaps it's her way of stopping herself from lashing out, but I doubt it. This is shock. I've seen it a thousand times.

My daughter continues to stare ahead, her face vacant – another look that I've seen a thousand times. I can imagine her mind is repeating everything I've just told her. The truth I've finally confessed. Me and Patrick, who Patrick is to her and, consequently, who Dylan is to her and what that means for the events that have taken place in her life over the past week, or even the past year, because I'm unsure how long these… these *relationships* have been in full swing.

I don't know what to do. I want to reach out and hold her hand, touch her arm, brush her glossy hair behind her ear, but I can't move. Either I'm mirroring my daughter's shock or it's fear – fear that if she remembers I'm here, she'll go nuts. Not that I could blame her, of course, I just don't want her to tell me to leave. It feels like it's been weeks rather than days since I knew she was okay, and although I know she's not, I want to be here for her. I need Rose to understand the lie I told when she was a small child was done out of love.

Rose opens her mouth; no sound escapes. She coughs lightly and turns her head away from me. The silence is suffocating.

Should I speak? Should I wait for her to speak first?

My insides feel like they're on fire. My body feels like it's encased in clay and I can't move. I can, obviously, but there's a small voice in my head warning me not to rock the boat. The truth is out there. I've confessed absolutely everything and apologised a hundred times. There's nothing more for me to say. I have to play the excruciating waiting game. This is Rose's time to digest everything – although, when I found out about her and Patrick, I almost threw up. Is this complete silence normal?

'So…' Rose speaks with an air of normalcy about her. 'You're telling me that I was in fact raped by *my* father, not *just* my boyfriend's father, and my boyfriend is actually my half-brother.'

I feel like I'm five again, tumbling from that tree, winded and gasping. Except this time, there's not even a hard ground beneath me to break my fall. Rape? Raped? No, Patrick said it was an affair. He had an affair with his son's girlfriend.

Rape.

Who…?

What…?

How…?

The questions build in my mind. None of them develop into anything more than stutters. I can't even contemplate asking them out loud, and my thoughts bring with them a lightness. Not in a happy giddy way, but a lightness that threatens to knock me out and snatch all consciousness from me. That is, until Rose speaks again, and I use the small amount of strength I have left to stay focused on her.

'I ran off to that glamping place because I felt bad. *I* felt guilty after what had happened between me and…' She pauses to catch her breath. 'Because Dylan found out. Well, he hadn't found out the truth, he knew a version of the truth that his father told him. I couldn't understand why Patrick told him. Then, when he dragged me from the beach, I could see how sad he was. I mean, he was angry at first, on the beach. Actually, I thought he might drown me at one point. After that, he was crushed. I didn't think he loved me that much. In all honesty, I thought Sheetal was after him, and Dylan loved the attention he got from her. It was so obvious to see. Then when he thought I'd been with his… Well, he was genuinely gutted. So, I had to wonder: did I lead his dad on? Did

I ask to be raped? Was I actually raped if Patrick told Dylan it was an affair? That's why I felt guilty. That's why I went away with Penny. I thought I did all of this.'

It's difficult to stay with Rose's thoughts as they jump from one thing to another; I'm sure she's making sense in her own mind, but I'm so confused. It's not helped by the crushing headache now pounding inside my skull. I can't stay quiet any more.

'Rose. Rose, I don't understand, sweetheart. Patrick told me that you were having an affair with him and–'

'And he fucking lied,' my daughter explodes. 'What, do you believe a rapist over your own child?'

Emotion has irrevocably kicked in and fully taken over Rose's character. Though she screamed, silent tears run down her face – she's no longer smooth and porcelain looking, but now red and aged, somehow. Without any warning, she's out of her seat, quickly pacing the room in a small circle, reminding me of a wild hyena circling its pray.

'So, Patrick told you and Dylan that we were having an affair. It's a lie. Yes, I found him attractive, and I thought I wanted something more to happen. When... when he finally did take it further, I told him to stop. I told him to stop–'

The wildness of the beast is visibly sucked from Rose's body as she falls to her knees, buries her head in her hands and sobs. Loud, shoulder-jerking sobs. I join my daughter on the floor and I cry too. I hold her tightly against my body. Although she doesn't embrace me in return, she also doesn't push me away and for that I'm thankful.

'None of this is your fault, sweetheart. I'm to blame. I'm the one who has lied to you since you were a little girl. If I'd been upfront from the start, you would have known. The name alone would have meant something to you when you came to this university. Or you would have tracked him down long before...' I shut up, hating my own words. 'Things just... just would have been different. I'm so sorry.'

I want to be able to speak better. I want to find the words that will explain how sorry I am, and that there are things we can do:

counselling, therapy, a holiday. I don't know. Something. Rose tilts her head up to me and the haggard look she had just moments before has gone. Her tear-stained face and brimming eyes make her look like a five-year-old. My five-year-old little girl.

What have I done?

Before I have time to hate myself further, or pass on some comforting words to my only child, the front room door bursts open which such force it slams against the wall. We jerk in each other's arms and turn to find a very handsome young man standing in the doorway, with a petrified-looking Sheetal dithering behind him. No formal introductions are needed. He looks too much like his father for me to not know this is Dylan.

'You.'

The huskiness of his voice only amplifies the venom in his tone further as he spits out that one word. I feel Rose's body go rigid beneath me; why does Dylan scare her so much? There's no need for her to worry because his hate isn't being aimed at her – his bulldog expression is aimed directly at me.

'You've ruined my family. My life. What the fuck is wrong with you?' he continues. He doesn't take a step further, though I can see his hands are balled into tight fists.

'Sheetal, you need to leave,' Rose says, and like some graceful dancer slipping through the air, she's out of my hold and standing between me and Dylan. 'This is… is… this doesn't concern you.'

Sheetal hesitates for a moment, no doubt feeling the suffocating tension as much as I am, but she says nothing. Dylan snakes further into the room and slams the door shut on Rose's housemate. I'm trying to fight the rising panic threatening to consume my entire body, but it's hopeless; the fear is too strong. Why am I fearful of two kids? Two students, for heaven's sake, and one of them is my own flesh and blood.

Probably because you've ruined their lives, as Dylan so clearly put it… a menacing voice echoes in my head.

'Dylan, listen.' Rose's voice is calm, whisper-like, and she takes a step towards him, slowly, as if trying to tame a crazy beast – ironic, really, when I just compared her to one. 'I'm sorry. I... I don't know what to say–'

'Your mum is a sick freak and you...' The spittle dances wildly from his mouth. 'It was bad enough when I thought you were a cheap slut who slept around with my father, but now... now... Oh my God, it's disgusting.'

A thought occurs to me. 'How do you know?'

Dylan snaps his head in my direction: his lips curled, his forehead creased as he frowns, his shoulders visibly slouched. This boy really is embodying the threat of a wild animal. It's important I don't say the wrong thing and antagonise him.

'My mum,' he answers, his tone still hoarse as if he's been shouting for hours. Or crying – that can have the same effect on a person's voice. It's then I notice the redness surrounding his eyelids, and my second thought is confirmed. 'Because it wasn't bad enough that you kept this dirty secret to yourself for over twenty years? My father had another child. Rose. Rose is his daughter.' He repeats the facts, but I get the feeling it's for his own benefit; he needs to hear the words again to make them real in his mind. 'Then you have to declare all to my mum while she's in hospital. Alone. Stuck in the bed, so she can't even get up and give you the bitch-slap that you deserve.'

As if that ignites a spark in him, Dylan lurches forward with his hand outstretched and wallops me around the face.

'Stop!' Rose yells.

'She deserves it.'

'Yes, she does, but you don't know when to flaming well stop.'

Rose has both our attention. Dylan flinches, as if it's him who received the smack, and I want to know what she means.

'Has he hit you, Rose?' I ask while pressing my palm to my cheek; it does nothing to extinguish the fire blazing on my skin.

'Mum, now is not the time. Dylan and I–'

'Don't give me that, young lady. Has this thug hit you before?'

Dylan groans and walks to the other side of the room. Rose says, 'He's not a thug, Mum. Jesus Christ, don't overreact. He got a bit rough with me on the beach last week when he found out, when Patrick told him we were having an affair. He's whacked you now because you fucking well deserve it.'

I cringe; my daughter's words hurt but she's right. An image of the beach is resurrected in my mind. 'Your ruby jewel…'

'What? How do you know I lost that? It was an accident. Dylan didn't mean to grab me so hard. He was just so hurt when he thought…'

'I found it,' I say. My words are distant, and my thoughts are already somewhere else. I turn to face the angry boy. 'Your father told you that he was having an affair with Rose? Why would he offer up that information voluntarily?'

The intensity in Dylan has diminished, and he whispers, 'Because I saw Rose leaving his office and I confronted him. I always had my suspicions that he fancied her. Oh my God, stop talking about this. It's making me feel sick.'

I disregard his pleas; this twisted mess has been ignored for long enough. 'So you and your father returned to the hospital, your mother flipped out and… and what? Did he still say it was just an affair?'

'What are you on about, you crazy woman?'

'Mum, stop.'

'Your father raped Rose. It wasn't an affair. It wasn't consensual. It was rape. That monster has you believing what he wants, to the extent that you think you can rough up my daughter.'

Dylan slides to the floor, grabbing chunks of his hair and balling his hands into fists. The sobs are quiet, but the shaking shoulders are rapid. The internal battle with his emotions is clear.

'I just… I don't know what to believe. I don't want to believe any of this. Affair, r-rape… This is all too much. How could you do this to us? I just need to find my father.'

My head is exploding. I feel as sick to my stomach as this poor boy. I push those feelings away for now, and my own angry beast crawls to the surface.

'So why did you come here?' I ask.

He shrugs, and part of me wants to kick his leg and awake the creature again because at least that side of him had something to say. Instead I crouch down, lightly touch his knee and tell him I'm sorry. It's not a lie – ha, there's my old friend irony again.

'Dylan, why did you think your dad would be here?'

He looks up, drags his sleeve along his nose and sniffs. 'Well, it was here or home. I took a chance and came here, thinking he would be as angry as I am and might come here looking for you or Rose. He just seemed... I don't know, I've never seen him like that. The way he left the hospital, I mean. I'm worried about him.'

'Your mum was angry with him?' I'm not sure if that's a question or a statement.

'Angry? No. She couldn't stop crying. She called him disgusting and a monster and... and so much more, but it wasn't out of anger. It was out of pure sadness. She said she never wanted to see him again. I could see the pain all over his face.'

I can imagine the look Dylan is talking about. For all his flaws, Patrick loves Sadie; it would almost be fairy-tale like if our lives weren't such a nightmare. That woman is his kryptonite.

'Where do you live, Dylan?'

'Yeah, right, as if I'm telling you. So you can do more damage to my family?'

Rose steps forward. 'If you're worried about him, just let my mum go. She started this mess. It's up to her to try to fix it. She can go back to the hospital with your dad and... I don't know, talk to your mum.'

There's something in Rose's voice. I can't pinpoint what it is, but I don't like it. She wants me to leave, that much I can tell, so I can only assume her calm exterior is false. She's as confused and angry and sad as the stooped little boy in front of me. If it's time away from me she needs, I'll give it to her for now. Anyway, her words do the trick and Dylan gives me his home address, and even fishes his car keys from his jeans pocket and tells me to take them.

Out in the fresh air, I'm surprised to see it is still daylight. That room was filled with such darkness, it feels as though it should be night-time. I'm grateful for the car. It will get me to Patrick quicker; not that I want to help him reconcile with his wife. No, of course I bloody don't want that. The beast in me – and we all have one, we just need to discover what will entice it to the surface of who we are; a lot of the time it's because our children are in danger or have already faced that danger – wants answers and retribution. I know I started all this. That one lie has spiralled out of control and ruined lives, more lives than I could have ever imagined. Patrick, he chose to be the monster he is. To treat my daughter the way he has… Okay, he didn't know she was his biological daughter – and that blame will always stay with me – but he knew she was someone's daughter. She was a woman who had the choice. He took that away from her. Snatched it away when she begged him not to. And as if that wasn't bad enough, he continued with the betrayal and lied to his son, telling him that Rose had consented, and caused his son to lash out at her. My anger towards Dylan is only dampened by the fact that I know it's Patrick's fault for what his son did.

I'm used to saving people's lives, but right now I want to take a life away.

That's an awful thought. I didn't mean to think it.

I was wrong. What the beast inside me wants is justice for my daughter.

Chapter thirty-five

I find Dylan's car easily enough – despite his only description being 'the black one outside' – as the left front wheel has mounted the kerb right outside Rose's house. The boy must have been in a rush to get to us… well, to get to me. I'd say he was in as much of a rush as I am to get to his father.

You're probably thinking: how the fuck do I know where to drive to? I don't live in Brighton but I'm screeching off in a kid's car on a mission. Well, luckily, that kid's car is a new, fancy-type one with a large digital screen – not just for the radio but also for the satnav. Dylan told me to hit the home button and his car would tell me exactly where to go… probably not in the *Knight Rider* manner I'd enjoy. I shouldn't let my mind wander.

It took only twenty minutes, and now I'm sitting outside Patrick's house. It's beautiful. A tall townhouse with the seafront as its view. Bay windows and plants are growing in the front garden. Why do things always seem idealistic when they're the things you want and can't have? Well, wanted. This life – being married to Patrick Malone – is the last thing I crave now. If only I'd known that before I decided to lie to Rose.

Before I can talk myself out of it, I jump from the fancy car and march up the path towards the door; that's when I notice the garage to the right of the house. The door is open, and Patrick's car is parked inside. I remember it from the day I saw him outside Rose's house. Surely that means he's here.

I bang on the front door, but it's quiet inside and there's no movement to make me think anyone is going to answer. Peeping through the letter box doesn't help. With the falling light behind me as the sun makes its descent and the lack of light inside, it's just a game of shadows and I can't make anything out. It certainly looks empty.

The sea breeze whips around my legs, almost as if it's trying to tug me away from the house. Walking away from the front door, I ignore my gut feeling. I ignore the gale, I ignore Dylan's car waiting for me, and I head to the right towards Patrick's garage.

There's a door inside the garage, and it leads into the house. I don't want to think about what I'm doing. If I ask myself too many questions, I'll talk myself out of what I'm about to do. Plus, it's not really breaking in if the door is unlocked and... Hey, there you go, it is.

The darkness from outside follows me into a utility room and then the kitchen. I want to turn the lights on, make some noise, call out Patrick's name, but a part of me also wants to just be – to wander around the house I could have had if things had been different. Wander around the house of the man who raped my daughter. Part of me just doesn't want anyone to know I'm here. I'm unsure of why, because I have no idea what I plan to do.

There's a glimmer of light up ahead of me, coming from a room on the left, down the hallway, so I follow it. The internal beast that was so active only thirty minutes previously seems to be cowering somewhat, and my overactive imagination is in play as I picture Patrick sitting in a large armchair facing the door with a gun in his hand. This was all a ruse: Dylan coming to the house, Rose telling me to go, the quiet and emptiness yet an open garage door inviting me. The three of them worked together to get me here. Revenge for telling Sadie the truth and for lying to everyone for all these years. Patrick will shoot me dead in his home the moment I enter that room.

Why would I? If I really think that's what's about to happen, why the hell would I go in?

To be proven right? To be proven wrong? Or because I think I deserve what's coming?

Stupidity or bravery?

Whatever makes me walk on, that's exactly what I do. As I cross the threshold, into a very grand family living room, I glimpse someone's legs and feet. Walking further into the room, and casting my eyes along the stiff figure on the floor, I realise it's Patrick. Next to him is an empty vodka bottle, but there's something more to this… something about how his body has fallen on the floor. There's more of a preparation to it, rather than a falling-down-blind-drunk look about it. Then there's the piece of paper in his hand – I can just make out the scribbled word 'Sadie' written on it – and the empty bottle of pills under the other hand.

This is it. This is what I wanted.

The man who ruined my life, who ruined my daughter's life, has saved me the trouble of seeking justice for myself.

I quickly crouch down to check his pulse. It's faint. Patrick is still with us. Who knows how long for, because who knows how long he's been lying here? Surely not much time has passed between him leaving the hospital and Dylan storming in on me and Rose, so there's plenty of time for Patrick to be saved. Isn't there? I'm sure a neighbour will come knocking, once they see the garage door open and his car parked up. They'll make the 999 call that will save him.

And then I'm backing away from him. I'm standing at the door again – this time, like a spy, or maybe even a hitman, waiting to watch the monster on the floor take his last breath. Yet I'm not a hitman at all because he chose to take his life. I did nothing.

Really? Is that true? Wasn't it my lie that created this?

Patrick Malone deserves to die. Surely you can't deny that? Look at what he's done in his life; from the affair with me in Scotland to raping a student in Brighton. And they're just the things we know about. Imagine what else he could have possibly done over the years. Even if he wasn't Rose's biological father, what he did to her was unforgiveable.

There are two sides to every story: she says he raped her, and he says they were having an affair.

I cringe at my own thoughts. How can I even say that to myself? Rose would never lie about a thing like that. This man lying on the floor is the epitome of scum and doesn't deserve a place in this world. Patrick Malone destroyed my life. He is a liar, a cheat, a monster…

Those words not only describe Patrick, but they also describe me. I am those things. I too have ruined lives. Who the hell am I to decide who gets to live or die? Isn't that why I became a paramedic? Human interaction, how people react, how people suffer and heal – that's what brought me to my profession. I never meant to destroy anyone's life with my lie.

But if I let Patrick die, that lie will probably die with him. I'd bet my life on Rose and Dylan, and even Sadie, not wanting anyone to know the truth. Therefore, no one will know I'm anything but the paramedic who saves people every day, and not the woman who told one monstrous lie that caused a half-brother and sister to have a relationship, a father to sleep with his daughter, a man to take his own life.

No, death is never the right kind of justice. Just because I have Rose back, it doesn't give me the authority to play God.

I grab my mobile from my pocket, dial the emergency services and balance the mobile between my shoulder and cheek. My voice is calm and professional, as if I'm working on a job I've been called to, and I relay all the information I have to the call handler while working on Patrick's airways.

* * *

Within half an hour the storm has been and gone. Dylan and Rose arrived at the house at the same time as the ambulance – they didn't know what Patrick had done, but they must have realised it wasn't a good idea to have two furious parents alone together. While waiting for the ambulance to arrive I kept my fingers on Patrick's pulse, as it was so weak. He lost it before the paramedics arrived, so I did what comes naturally to me and started CPR – the old-fashioned mouth-to-mouth way. I saved his life. Then I gladly handed him over to the Brighton paramedic duo – luckily not the same two I already saw today.

Dylan went to the hospital with his father, of course – the poor boy now has both parents there – and I find myself standing on the seafront with Rose. She's quiet, but she's brooding, I can tell. There's another storm on the way. It's brewing inside of her and the atmosphere between us feels as dark as the overcast clouds swirling above our heads.

'Rose, is there anything you want to–'

'Do you still love him?' she interrupts.

'Who? Patrick?' I snort. I don't know why I made that noise – am I trying to laugh off her question or is because I feel so numb inside that I'm incapable of answering the question? 'Don't be so ridiculous.' This seems to be the safest reply.

'Then why did you save him?'

I sigh, understanding where she's going with this. 'Because that's my job, sweetheart.'

'No,' she almost yells. 'You're a mother before you're a paramedic. Your job is to look after me, make sure I'm safe, not strangers and certainly not scum like *Patrick Malone*.'

'Rose, darling–'

'No, Mum.' She swivels around to look directly at me, her lips turned down in disgust, her cheeks flushed bright red, her forehead furrowed – a face contorted with rage. 'As if it isn't bad enough that I fancied this man, that I was attracted to my own fucking father. Then to have him… have him force himself on me. To have him… tear down my knickers.' Fresh gushing tears are added to her rage. 'All of that and then… I don't even want to think about me and Dylan and what that means. I will never forgive you for lying to me.'

With that final blow, Rose turns on her heels, running away from me. The exhaustion could be overlooked. I could leg it after her, pleading and begging. I know there's no point. After everything she just said, I'd be mad not to realise she needs some time. Time away from me. How long, exactly, I really don't know, but the worst thing I can do is push her. I can't force her to talk to me, or to see me, and I shouldn't have to. She'll come back to me when she's ready, when she's calmed down, and I can explain everything to her. The reason I told this bloody lie was all for her. My own words come back to haunt me – *I have to continue with this lie because I'm not about to ruin my daughter's life* – yet even though I believed what I'd done was the right thing when Rose was a child, it's actually the exact thing that has ruined my daughter.

I have to admit that. I have to embrace my mistakes if I ever hope to make Rose understand. What I did was so terribly wrong. I see that now more than I ever thought I could. Surely, in time, my daughter will realise that too, and she'll let me defend myself, won't she?

Rose is safe. At the moment, that is what really matters: that I have Rose back in my life and, soon enough, we'll be able to restore our relationship to what it was. She will forgive me, and I know I will never ever lie to my daughter again.

Chapter thirty-six

It's been a week and a half and Rose hasn't returned any of my calls or replied to any of my messages. It's like my life is stuck in an unpleasant loop, mocking me, taking away the one important thing to me. Again.

Part of me knows that I had to tell the truth; it was cruel and unfair and wrong to let them all live in that lie. I understand that, I really do. Yet there is a slither of something inside me, a piece of me that wants to hold on to my life when it was simpler, and when Rose called me every day, even sent me Snapchat videos to make me smile. My daughter was back in my life, so did I really have to tell the truth? If I hadn't, it could have been Rose curled up on the sofa with me instead of Adele.

My crew member knows everything. It would seem that now I've opened up about my dark secret, I can't shut up. I'll tell anyone who's interested that I'm an evil liar who wrecked her daughter's life.

'You're not evil,' Adele says. 'Flaming hell, Abi, how could you have ever known that that one lie would lead to… to this destruction.' I throw her a look and drain my glass of wine. 'Okay, destruction is a harsh word, but I'm not here to sugar-coat things.'

I roll my eyes and refill both our glasses. 'No? Why are you here then?'

'To make sure you're okay. Dave is really worried about you. Everyone at the station is. How long do you plan on staying on sick leave?'

'There's things I need to sort out, Adele. I can't just slip back into my old routine. Things aren't how they used to be. Rose could come home at any time, looking for answers and wanting to understand what happened all those years ago. Plus, there's my mum. I haven't visited her or returned any of the calls from the hospice. Oh my God, do you see how evil I really am?'

Adele's lips twist like she's snarling, and her nostrils flare, but it's not in an evil looking way. 'Well then, girl, you need to get out of your pyjamas. Maybe even have a shower too. Stop feeling sorry for yourself and moping around.' I want to interrupt, tell her to stop talking and bossing me around, but she places her palm in front of my face and continues. 'Listen to me. Rose will not come to you. For heaven's sake, some twisted shit went down in Brighton, she's a broken woman and, at the moment anyway, you're the cause of that pain.'

'I thought something awful happened to her–'

'And it did.'

It's my turn to flare my nostrils. 'I meant I thought she died.'

'Abi, a part of her probably did die that night. She sees you as being the driving force behind that. It's been just over a week since she discovered the truth; that's nothing in terms of moving on or coming to terms with things. Give her time. For now, visit your mum, come back to work and focus on getting yourself back to normal. You can't help your daughter in this state. Oh, and have a wash will you, woman?'

There's a lightness to her tone. She's trying to make me laugh, but that I can't do, so I offer her a small smile of some kind and hope she recognises that I'm grateful.

'You know, Dave really fancies the arse off you, Abi.'

'What?' I'm thrown by Adele's curveball.

'Oh, come on, you can't tell me you really haven't noticed. If you asked him out for a drink, he would jump at the chance. Maybe you should.'

'You've got to be kidding me. Are we really back here again?'

Adele puts the wine glass down and turns to face me full-on; it's a bit intense. 'Look, I don't mean marry the guy, but I think it's time you had some fun in your life again. If you won't do that – if you won't have a cheeky date with Dave – then at least talk to someone about all this. A professional, I mean, not just me, as understanding as I am.'

'You mean like a therapist… really?'

'I just mean you need to offload all this guilt and sadness that you have bouncing around inside of you. It's no good for man or beast. You have to learn to smile again.'

'I just did.'

She groans. 'Uh, not that half-hearted weak smirk you just showed me. I mean properly smile, belly laugh, enjoy life.'

I finish the wine in my glass before I put it down, then rub both hands over my face. 'Adele, how can you say that to me? I told you I almost left a man to die and you're telling me to go out and belly laugh.'

'Almost.'

'What?' My head is pounding.

'You almost left him, Abi, but you didn't, and that's the point. You are a good woman. Yes, you told one hell of a lie but that was over twenty years ago. You have to forgive yourself. How can you expect Rose to forgive you if you can't? You're not evil. The lie you told was out of love for your daughter; you thought it was best if she didn't know. You planned to tell her the truth much sooner, and it all just ran away with you. That's the thing about lies – it's so easy to start believing them yourself. These things happen. In the end, you told the truth, despite it meaning the worst for you, and you chose to save Patrick's life. There's nothing evil about you.'

I exhale deeply. 'Wow, Adele, fancy a new job as that therapist you were talking about?'

She giggles and I grin widely. No, not a belly laugh, but the smile is genuine, so that's a start.

'Okay, I hear what you're saying, I really do. There's no way I'm ready for dating. No, no, I'm really not. But I will get some help. You're right, I need to talk to someone. A counsellor, or therapist, or… someone. That will help, right? Maybe Rose could do the same. We wouldn't have to do it together. It would help her too.

With what she's been through…' I reach for my phone, which has sat silent on the coffee table for hours.

'What, now?' Adele asks. 'You have the number for a therapist on speed dial?'

'Don't be daft. I'm going to send Rose a text. And don't tell me to give her space. I am – well, I will – but I'm just going to send this last message first.'

Adele doesn't stop me. Perhaps it's the determined look I know I must have in my eyes. Rose might have given up on me, but I won't give up on her; she's my daughter. I'll invite her round, tell her my idea about us both seeing a counsellor and she'll see. She'll see that I'm seriously sorry for what I did. The lie I told has meant some awful things have happened to her… to Dylan and Patrick too. I acknowledge that, but I won't let this tragedy define me. I'm not an evil person. Adele is right, it was a lie born out of love for my daughter, and it's a lie I'll put right with that same love for her.

No matter how long it takes, no matter how many times I have to say sorry and no matter how many times I have to retell the truth, I'll make sure it's not only strangers I'm saving. I'll make sure that no more lives are destroyed because of the lie I told.

Epilogue

One month later

It takes every ounce of strength in me to stand up and walk towards the altar. As I pass the dark oak coffin on my way to the podium that the priest has just vacated for me, my entire body shivers. I hope no one behind me noticed. The church is packed, unsurprisingly.

After everything that has happened in the last five weeks or so, this is the last place I want to be. Well, obviously no one ever wants to attend a funeral – but my overwhelming desire not to be here is magnified by all the lies and cheating and... and all the hate that's been spread around. Most days I just want to lock myself away and cry. However, my counsellor said that my being here was instrumental in my recovery. In order for me to move forward, I need to say goodbye to my mother. I need some closure.

If only she knew the truth.

Another chapter in my life is being built on the foundation of a terrible lie.

'My mum is... was... an amazing woman,' I spurt out as soon as my mouth reaches the microphone; my voice echoes around the high beamed ceiling, unnerving me, and everyone's eyes are on me. I search for a familiar face to calm me and, when I find it, I continue. 'Throughout her life she helped many different people in many different ways, so I'm not surprised at all that so many of you are here today.'

The babble endures, but I hardly recognise my own voice. I'm just reading from the piece of paper that I wrote my notes on last night. There's nothing too personal; not about me anyway. I don't think I could write anything about me, about what I've done and who I eventually grew up to be. And if I can't say anything truthful about myself, I would rather say nothing at all. That's my new motto, after everything that's happened.

It's a lovely service. Most people say that, don't they? Why wouldn't someone's final farewell be lovely and peaceful? No one really understands the circumstances behind my mother's death, so there's no need for suspicion and whispers at this funeral.

It was lovely of the care home to assist my grandmother today. It wouldn't have been the same if she wasn't here; in fact, I think she's the real reason that I came. As I push her wheelchair away from the grave, and the fresh mound of earth that will soon bury my mother in the ground forever, I look back and scan all the flowers: the roses and lilies and bouquets from her colleagues. I never knew so many people cared about my mother. Neither did she actually. I was all she had in this world. That's what she thought, so it's a shame she lied to me my entire life. It's her fault.

This is all her fault.

For as much as it has pleased Almighty God – the priest's words play again my mind – *to take out of this world the soul of Abigail Nora Quinn, we therefore commit her body to the ground. Earth to earth, ashes to ashes, dust to dust.*

I can't remember what he said after that. I was too focused on ensuring the coffin – and her lying body – was sent down into that deep, muddy hole where she belongs.

You probably think I'm the evil one, don't you? Would it matter if I promised that it hadn't been my intention to kill her? I *loved* my mother – yes, past tense and not because she's dead – but Jesus Christ was she overbearing and suffocating. Then, when I found out I had been raped by my father because of *her*, something inside me snapped.

Receiving that final text message from her was the last straw. I knew then that she would never leave me alone. Every time I saw her face, heard her voice, even read a message from her, I was transported back to that office, back to when Patrick forced my clothes away from my body, back to when Patrick – to when my *father* – touched me, despite me begging him to stop. When she first told me the truth, I was sickened. That feeling soon passed. The days following my mother's confession, I felt anger and hatred, resentment and fury, and, strangely enough, it wasn't aimed at Patrick – though what he had done to me was scandalous no matter who I was – but all the wrath that bubbled up inside me was at her. My mother, the liar.

I did go round to see her that night, like she asked me to in her text message, with nothing in my mind other than to tell her to leave me the fuck alone. To explain that seeing her and speaking to her brought the nightmares back. But then, something happened.

We started arguing. Mum and I never shouted at one another. I had never needed to; that woman did whatever I asked her to and gave me whatever I wanted. But she was mad too – mad at herself for lying, mad at being found out, mad at not being able to control the situation.

She was screaming like a fucking banshee that *I* didn't understand how hard it was for *her* to imagine what the love of her life, my father, had done to me. In that moment, the rubber band inside me, holding all my emotions together, snapped. I broke. I shattered like glass.

How dare she say that to me. To me, the woman who suffered because of *her* lie.

I pushed her. Shoved her so hard that I actually heard her body crash against each step as she tumbled down. I heard her head smack against the banister before one final crack on the uncarpeted floor. It was instant. Watching from the top of the stairs, I knew she was gone. The blood oozing from her head was the first telltale sign. The next was checking her pulse; yes, I went through the motions, it was easier that way. Then, when I called 999 there were fewer lies to tell. It also helped that there were three bottles of wine in the bin.

It was a terrible accident.

Mum always found it amazing that so many of her patients faced the same accidents yet came out the other end with such different injuries. She had said, 'How can some people walk away from a four-car collision with merely a scratch, but others can innocently trip over, bang their head and die instantly? How do cancer and dementia and multiple sclerosis attack people's bodies in such different ways that it gives each of them a completely unique quality – or lack thereof – of life?' I now add: how can someone fall down the stairs and break a leg or an arm, yet a paramedic can tumble down one flight and bash their head and neck in such a way that it's a fatal accident?

It was such a terrible accident.

At first, the police assumed I should have been able to save my mum. Stop the bleeding, perform CPR, probably fucking operate on her because, you know, I'm Rose the Paramedic's Daughter. And that's how it's presented, like a full name: it's my first name and surname. Like she defines me. Growing up was different. I was young and gullible and thought that title brought me something. Power? Respect? Now I know it means nothing. It's just another way for me to be controlled.

You know, I'm more than who my mum was – or what she did. I'm a student, I'm an aspiring writer, I'm... I'm... for crying out loud, I'm a woman who was raped by their father, a man I was attracted to, a man I wanted to kiss, a man who, at first anyway, was someone I lusted over and dreamt about. Most importantly, a man I thought was my boyfriend's father – not mine.

So, even if I could have saved her, I wouldn't have. Why would I? The push wasn't an accident. Yes, I saw red, but I knew exactly what I was doing. I thought it would free me, free me from the anger and hatred that I had been directing towards her. It just redirected it. To Patrick. To Dylan. But mostly, to my grandmother. The old woman knew. She told me last night before the funeral, said she needed to get it off her chest, to feel free. *Free.* Well, sadly I don't have that luxury to indulge in, Gran. She knew the truth. She could have saved me, but she chose to stick by my mother's lie – even before the blasted dementia.

The hospice manager has allowed my grandmother to stay with me tonight, at my mother's home. He said that it would be comforting for us to be together at this awful time. *Comforting...* yeah, right. I hope there isn't another *awful* accident tonight.

My mother has destroyed me. My mother's lie has brought my internal beast to the surface.

THE END

ACKNOWLEDGEMENTS

This is the hardest part of the writing journey for me. I have so many people to thank – especially for this book, which has been a long time coming.

The Paramedic's Daughter is a book I've wanted to write for some time now. Abi, mainly, has been brewing in my mind for well over a year. Her story and experiences have changed dramatically since I began writing, and that's the joy of letting the characters take over. However, with that joy comes the need to be authentic – even more so because of the profession she's in. For that authenticity, I have to thank my long-time friend Laura Fraser. The paramedic herself who fact-checked the entire book, while organising her wedding – you are a true star and deserve all the monkey hugs. I must also thank Jo Edwards who came to my rescue when a specific part of the book needed clarifying – it's not what you know, it's who you know.

To the team at Bloodhound Books, you are amazing. Betsy, I can't thank you enough for helping me to have confidence in my writing voice. To Sumaira, Alexina, Heather and Fred for the friendships, encouragement, laughs and patience – big thanks. To my cover designer, editor and proofreader, thank you for helping me make this book shine.

This book is very different to my DI Hamilton series, but it was greeted with the same enthusiasm and excitement from a very special group of people. So it's with a lot of love that I thank the bloggers who took part in the tour: Kat Everett, Noelle

Holten, Shell Baker, Sarah Hardy, Claire Knight, Kate Moloney, Kim Nash, Kaisha Holloway and Lesley Budge, as well as all the amazing people in my ARC group. Your love of reading, and the continued support you give, blows me away.

Special mention to my beta readers Maria Lee, Audrey Gibson and Mark Fearn, and also to Tammie Ferguson who won a competition on my author Facebook page to name a character. Thanks to you, we have Sadie.

To my dear friends who lift my spirits on a daily basis, who show me nothing but support and encouragement and who are always checking in to see how the writing is coming along or how the editing is going – I send you 'good vibes only'.

Lastly, to my amazing family. I wouldn't be able to continue doing what I love if it weren't for you. Abi and Rose's relationship may have been a strained one – to say the least – but I'm thankful every day for the bond I have with my mum; the woman who taught me everything I know, the woman who made me who I am today and the woman who puts her life on hold to help me whenever she can. Just as I was finishing the last draft of this book, we had a new arrival join us – five days earlier than expected – and so three became four. Daniel, Leo and Sofia, this is for you.

Printed in Great Britain
by Amazon

43910548R00125